KU-351-611

First published in 1971
Reprinted in 1984, 1985

Published by Deans International Publishing
52–54 Southwark Street, London SE1 1UA
A Division of The Hamlyn Publishing Group Limited
London · New York · Sydney · Toronto

ISBN 0 603 03281 8

Printed and bound by Purnell and Sons (Book Production) Ltd.,
Paulton, Bristol.
Member of BPCC plc

THE MAGIC FARAWAY TREE

by
Enid Blyton

DEANS
INTERNATIONAL
PUBLISHING

THE ENID BLYTON TRUST FOR CHILDREN

We hope you will enjoy the stories in this book. Please think for a moment about those children who are too ill to do the exciting things you and your friends do.

Help them by sending a donation, large or small, to THE ENID BLYTON TRUST FOR CHILDREN. The Trust will use all your gifts to help children who are sick or handicapped and need to be made happy and comfortable.

Please send your postal order or cheque to:
The Enid Blyton Trust for Children,
Lee House,
London Wall,
London, EC2Y 5AS

Thank you very much for your help.

CONTENTS

I

DICK COMES TO STAY

Once upon a time there were three children, Jo, Bessie and Fanny. They lived with their mother and father in a little cottage deep in the country. The girls had to help their mother in the house, and Jo helped his father in the garden.

Now, one day their mother had a letter. She didn't very often have letters, so the children wondered what it was about.

"Listen!" she said. "This is something quite exciting for you. Your cousin Dick is coming to stay with us!"

"Ooh!" said all the children, pleased. Dick was about the same age as Jo. He was a merry boy, rather naughty, and it would be such fun to have him.

"He can sleep with me in my little bedroom!" said Jo. "Oh, Mother, what fun! When is he coming?"

"To-morrow," said Mother. "You girls can put up a little bed for him in Jo's room, and, Jo, you must make room for Dick's things in your cupboard. He is going to stay quite a long time, because his mother is ill and can't look after him."

The three children flew upstairs to get Jo's room ready for Dick as well.

"I say! What will Dick say when we tell him about the Enchanted Wood and the Faraway Tree?" cried Jo.

"And what will he say when we show him our friends there—Silky, and old Moon-Face, and the dear old deaf Saucepan Man, and everyone!" said Bessie.

"He *will* get a surprise!" said Fanny.

They got everything ready for their cousin. They put up a little camp-bed for him, and found some blankets. They put a cushion for a pillow. They made room in Jo's cupboard and chest of drawers for Dick's things. Then they looked out of the window. It looked on to a dark, thick wood, whose trees waved in the wind, not far from the bottom of the garden.

"The Enchanted Wood!" said Bessie softly. "What marvellous adventures we have had there. Maybe Dick will have some, too."

Dick arrived the next day. He came in the carrier's cart, with a small bag of clothes. He jumped down and hugged the children's mother.

"Hallo, Aunt Polly!" he said. "It's good of you to have me. Hallo, Jo! I say, aren't Bessie and Fanny big now? It's lovely to be with you all again."

The children took him up to his room. The girls unpacked his bag and put his things neatly away in the cupboard and the chest. They showed him the bed he was to sleep on.

"I expect I shall find it rather dull here after living in London," said Dick, putting his hair-brushes on the little dressing-table. "It seems so quiet. I shall miss the noise of buses and trams."

"You won't find it dull!" said Jo. "My word,

Dick, we've had more adventures since we've been here than ever we had when we lived in a big town."

"What sort of adventures?" asked Dick in surprise. "It seems such a quiet place that I shouldn't have thought there was even a small adventure to be found!"

The children took Dick to the window. "Look, Dick," said Jo. "Do you see that thick, dark wood over there, backing on to the lane at the bottom of our garden?"

"Yes," said Dick. "It seems quite ordinary to me, except that the leaves of the trees seem a darker green than usual."

"Well, listen, Dick—that's the *Enchanted Wood!*" said Bessie.

Dick's eyes opened wide. He stared at the wood. "You're making fun of me!" he said at last.

"No, we're not," said Fanny. "We mean what we say. Its name is the Enchanted Wood—and it *is* enchanted. And oh, Dick, in the middle of it is the most wonderful tree in the world!"

"What sort of tree?" asked Dick, feeling quite excited.

"It's a simply enormous tree," said Jo. "Its top goes right up to the clouds—and oh, Dick, at the top of it is always some strange land. You can go there by climbing up the top branch of the Faraway Tree, going up a little ladder through a hole in the big cloud that always lies on the top of the tree—and there you are in some peculiar land!"

"I don't think I believe you," said Dick. "You are making it all up."

"Dick! We'll take you there and show you what we mean," said Bessie. "It's all quite true. Oh, Dick, we've had such exciting adventures at the top of the Faraway Tree. We've been to the Rocking Land, and the Birthday Land."

"And the Land of Take-What-You-Want and the Land of the Snowman," said Fanny. "You just can't think how exciting it all is."

"And, Dick, all kinds of queer folk live in the trunk of the Faraway Tree," said Jo. "We've lots of good friends there. We'll take you to them one day. There's a dear little fairy called Silky, because she has such a mass of silky gold hair."

"And there's Moon-Face, with a big round face like the moon! He's a darling!" said Bessie.

"And there's funny old Mister Watzisname," said Fanny.

"What's his real name?" asked Dick in surprise.

"Nobody knows, not even himself," said Jo. "So everyone calls him Mister Watzisname. Oh, and there is the old Saucepan Man. He's always hung around with kettles and saucepans and things, and he's so deaf that he always hears everything wrong."

Dick's eyes began to shine. "Take me there," he begged. "Quick, take me! I can't wait to see all these exciting people."

"We can't go till Mother says she doesn't need us in the house," said Bessie. "But we *will* take you – of course we will."

"And, Dick, there's a slippery slip, a slide that goes right down the inside of the tree from the top to the bottom," said Fanny. "It belongs to Moon-Face. He lends people cushions to slide down on."

"I do want to go down that slide," said Dick, getting terribly impatient. "Why do you tell me all these things if you can't take me to see them now? I'll never be able to sleep to-night! Good gracious! My head feels in a whirl already to think of the Faraway Tree and Moon-Face and Silky and the slippery-slip."

"Dick, we'll take you as soon as ever we can," promised Jo. "There's no hurry. The Faraway

Tree is always there. We never, never know what land is going to be at the top. We have to be very careful sometimes because there might be a dangerous land – one that we couldn't get away from!"

A voice came from downstairs. "Children! Are you going to stay up all the day? I suppose you don't want any tea? What a pity – because I have made some scones for you and put out some strawberry jam!"

Four children raced down the stairs. Scones and strawberry jam! Gracious, they weren't going to miss those. Good old Mother – she was always thinking of some nice little treat for them.

"Jo, Father wants you to dig up some potatoes for him after tea," said Mother. "Dick can help you. And, Bessie and Fanny, I want you to finish my ironing for me, because I have to take some mended clothes to Mrs. Harris, and she lives such a long way away."

The children had been rather hoping to go out and take Dick to the Enchanted Wood. They looked disappointed. But they said nothing, because they knew that in a family everyone had to help when they could.

Mother saw their disappointed faces and smiled. "I suppose you want to take Dick to see those peculiar friends of yours," she said. "Well now, listen – if you are good children to-day, and do the jobs you have to do, I'll give you a whole day's holiday to-morrow! Then you may take your dinner and your tea and go to visit any friends you like. How would you like that?"

"Oh, Mother, thank you!" cried the children in delight.

"A whole day!" said Bessie. "Why, Dick, we can show you everything!"

"And maybe let you peep into whatever land is at the top of the Faraway Tree," whispered Fanny. "Oh, what fun!"

So they did their work well after tea and looked forward to the next day. Dick dug hard, and Jo was pleased with him. It was going to be fun to have a cousin with them, able to work and play and enjoy everything, too!

When they went to bed that night they left the doors of their rooms open so that they might call to one another.

"Sleep well, Dick!" called Bessie. "I hope it's fine to-morrow! What fun we shall have!"

"Good night, Bessie!" called back Dick. "I can't tell you how I'm longing for to-morrow. I know I shan't be able to sleep to-night!"

But he did—and so did all the others. When Mother came up at ten o'clock she peeped in at the children, and not one was awake.

Jo woke first next day. He sat up and looked out of the window. The sun streamed in, warm and bright. Jo's heart jumped for joy. He leaned over to Dick's bed and shook him.

"Wake up!" he said. "It's to-morrow now—and we're going to the Enchanted Wood!"

II

OFF TO THE ENCHANTED WOOD

The children ate their breakfast quickly. Mother told Bessie and Fanny to cut sandwiches for themselves and to take a small chocolate cake from the larder.

"You can take a packet of biscuits, too," she said, "and there are apples in that dish over there. If you are hungry when you come home to-night I will bake you some potatoes in the oven, and you can eat them in their skins with salt and butter."

"Oooh, Mother—we *shall* be hungry!" said Jo at once. "Hurry up with those sandwiches, Bessie and Fanny. We want to start off as soon as possible."

"Now don't be too late home, or I shall worry," said Mother. "Look after your cousin, Jo."

"Yes, I will," promised Jo.

At last everything was ready. Jo packed the food into a leather bag and slung it over his shoulder. Then the four of them set off to the Enchanted Wood.

It didn't take them long to get there. A narrow ditch was between the lane and the wood.

"You've got to jump over the ditch, Dick," said Jo. They all jumped over. Dick stood still when he was in the wood.

"What a strange noise the leaves of the trees make," he said. "It's as if they were talking to one another—telling secrets."

"Wisha, wisha, wisha, wisha," whispered the trees.

"They *are* talking secrets," said Bessie. "And do you know, Dick—if the trees have any message for us, we can hear it by pressing our left ears to the trunks of the trees! Then we *really* hear what they say."

"Wisha-wisha-wisha-wisha," said the trees.

"Come on," said Jo impatiently. "Let's go to the Faraway Tree."

They all went on—and soon came to the queer magic tree. Dick stared at it in the greatest astonishment.

"Why, it's simply ENORMOUS!" he said. "I've never seen such a big tree in my life. And you can't possibly see the top. Goodness gracious! What kind of tree is it? It's got oak leaves, and yet it doesn't really seem like an oak."

"It's a funny tree," said Bessie. "It may grow acorns and oak leaves for a little way—and then suddenly you notice that it's growing plums. Then another day it may grow apples or pears. You just never know. But it's all very exciting."

"How do you climb it?" asked Dick. "In the ordinary way?"

"Well, we will to-day," said Jo, "because we want to show you our friends who live inside the tree. But sometimes there's a rope that is let down the tree, and we can go up quickly with the help of that. Or sometimes Moon-Face lets down a cushion on the end of a rope and then pulls us up one by one."

He swung himself up into the tree, and the others followed. After a bit Dick gave a shout. "I say! It's most extraordinary! This tree is growing nuts now! Look!"

Sure enough it was. Dick picked some and cracked them. They were hazel nuts, ripe and sweet. Everyone had some and enjoyed them.

Now when they had all got very high up indeed, Dick was most surprised to see a little window in the trunk of the Faraway Tree.

"Goodness – does somebody live just here?" he called to the others. "Look – there's a window here. I'm going to peep in."

"You'd better not!" shouted Jo. "The Angry Pixie lives there, and he hates people peeping in."

But Dick felt so curious that he just *had* to peep in. The Angry Pixie was at home. He was filling his kettle with water, when he looked up and saw Dick's surprised face at his window. Nothing made the pixie so angry as to see people looking at him. He rushed to the window at once and flung it open.

"Peeping again!" he shouted. "It's too bad! All day and night people come peeping. Take that!"

He emptied the kettle of water all over poor Dick. Then he slammed his window and drew the curtains across. Jo, Bessie and Fanny couldn't help laughing.

"I told you not to peep in at the Angry Pixie," said Jo, wiping Dick with his hanky. "He's nearly always in a bad temper. Oh, and by the way, Dick,

I must warn you about something else. There's an old woman who lives high up in the tree who is always washing. She empties the water down the tree, and it comes slish-sloshing down. You'll have to look out for that or you'll get wet."

Dick looked up the tree as if he half expected the water to come tumbling down at once.

"Come on," said Bessie. "We'll come to where the Owl lives soon. He's a friend of Silky's, and sometimes brings us notes from her."

The owl was fast asleep. He usually only woke up at night-time. Dick peered in at his window and saw the big owl asleep on a bed. He couldn't help laughing.

"I *am* enjoying all this," he said to Fanny. "It's quite an adventure."

The children climbed higher, and came to a broad branch. "There's a dear little yellow door, with a knocker and a bell!" cried Dick in surprise, staring at the door set neatly in the trunk of the tree. "Who lives there?"

"Our friend Silky," said Jo. "Ring the bell and she'll open the door."

Dick rang the little bell and heard it go ting-a-ling inside. Footsteps pattered to the door. It opened, and a pretty little elf looked out. Her hair hung round her face like a golden mist.

"Hallo, Silky!" cried Jo. "We've come to see you – and we've brought our cousin, Dick, who has come to live with us. He's having a lovely time exploring the Faraway Tree."

"How do you do, Dick?" said Silky, holding out

her small hand. Dick shook hands shyly. He thought Silky was the loveliest creature he had ever seen.

"I'll come with you if you are going to visit Moon-Face," said Silky. "I want to borrow some jam from him. I'll take some Pop Biscuits with me, and we'll have them in Moon-Face's house."

"Whatever are Pop Biscuits?" asked Dick, in surprise.

"Wait and see!" said Jo with a grin.

They all went up the tree again. Soon they heard a funny noise. "That's old Mister Watzisname snoring," said Jo. "Look – there he is!"

Sure enough, there he was, sitting in a comfortable chair, his hands folded over his big tummy, and his mouth wide open.

"How I'd love to pop something into his open mouth!" said Dick at once.

"Yes, that's what everybody feels," said Jo. "Moon-Face and Silky once popped some acorns in – didn't you, Silky? And Watzisname was very angry. He threw Moon-Face up through the hole in the cloud, and landed him into the strange country there."

"Where's the old Saucepan Man?" asked Bessie. "He is usually with his friend, Mister Watzisname."

"I expect he has gone to see Moon-Face," said Silky. "Come on. We'll soon be there."

As they went up the tree, Silky suddenly stopped. "Listen," she said. They all listened. They heard a curious noise – "slishy-sloshy-slishy-sloshy"—coming nearer and nearer.

"It's Dame Washalot's dirty water coming!" yelled Jo. "Get under a branch, everyone."

Dick wasn't as quick as the others. They all hid under big boughs—but poor old Dick wasn't quite under his when the water came pouring down the tree. It tumbled on to his head and went down his neck. Dick was very angry. The others were sorry, but they thought it was very funny, too.

"Next time I climb this tree I'll wear a bathing-dress," said Dick, trying to wipe himself dry. "Really, I think somebody ought to stop Dame Washalot pouring her water away like that. How disgusting!"

"Oh, you'll soon get used to it, and dodge the water easily," said Jo. On they all went up the tree again, and at last came almost to the top. There they saw a door in the trunk of the tree, and from behind the door came the sound of voices.

"That's Moon-Face and the old Saucepan Man," said Jo, and he banged on the door. It flew open and Moon-Face looked out. His big round face beamed with smiles when he saw who his visitors were.

"Hallo, hallo, hallo," he said. "Come along in. The Saucepan Man is here."

Everyone went into Moon-Face's curious round room. There was a large hole in the middle of it, which was the beginning of the slippery-slip, the wonderful slide that went round and round down the inside of the tree, right to the bottom. Moon-Face's furniture was arranged round the inside of the tree trunk, and it was all curved to fit the curve of the tree. His bed was curved, the chairs were curved, the sofa and the stove. It was very queer.

Dick stared at it all in the greatest surprise. He really felt as if he must be in a dream. He saw somebody very queer sitting on the sofa.

It was the old Saucepan Man. He really was a very curious sight. He was hung all round with saucepans and kettles, and he wore a saucepan for a hat. You could hardly see anything of him except his face, hands and feet, because he was so hung about with saucepans and things. He made a tremendous clatter whenever he moved.

"Who's that?" he said, looking at Dick.

"This is Dick," said Jo, and Dick went forward to shake hands.

The Saucepan Man was very deaf, though he did sometimes hear quite well. But he nearly always heard everything wrong, and sometimes he was very funny.

"Chick?" he said. "Well, that's a funny name for a boy."

"Not Chick, but DICK!" shouted Moon-Face.

"Stick?" said the Saucepan Man, shaking hands. "Good morning, Stick. I hope you are well."

Dick giggled. Moon-Face got ready to shout again, but Silky quickly handed him her bag of Pop Biscuits. "Don't get cross with him," she said. "Look–let's all have some Pop Biscuits. They are fresh made to-day. And, oh, Moon-Face, do tell us–what land is at the top of the Faraway Tree to-day?"

"The Land of Topsy-Turvy," said Moon-Face. "But I don't advise you to go there. It's most uncomfortable."

"Oh, do let's," cried Dick. "Can't we just *peep* at it?"

"We'll see," said Jo, giving him a Pop Biscuit. "Eat this, Dick."

Pop Biscuits were lovely. Dick put one in his mouth and bit it. It went pop! at once–and he found his mouth full of sweet honey from the middle of the biscuit.

"Delicious!" he said. "I'll have another. I say, Jo–DO let's take our lunch up into the land of Topsy-Turvy. Oh, do, do!"

III

THE LAND OF TOPSY-TURVY

"What is Topsy-Turvy Land like?" asked Jo, taking another Pop Biscuit.

"Never been there," said Moon-Face. "But I should think it's quite safe, really. It's only just come there, so it should stay for a while. We could go up and see what it's like and come down again if we don't like it. Silky and I and Saucepan will come with you, if you like."

Moon-Face turned to the Saucepan Man, who was enjoying his fifth Pop Biscuit.

"Saucepan, we're going up the ladder," he said. "Are you coming?"

"Humming?" said Saucepan, looking all round as if he thought there might be bees about. "No, I didn't hear any humming."

"I said, are you COMING?" said Moon-Face.

"Oh, *coming*!" said Saucepan. "Of course I'm coming. Are we going to take our lunch?"

"Yes," said Moon-Face, going to a curved door that opened on to a tiny larder. "I'll see what I've got. Tomatoes. Plums. Ginger snaps. Ginger beer. I'll bring them all."

He put them into a basket. Then they all went out of the funny, curved room on to the big branch outside. Moon-Face shut his door.

Jo led the way up to the very top of the Faraway Tree. Then suddenly Dick gave a shout of astonishment.

"Look!" he cried. "There's an enormous white cloud above and around us. Isn't it queer!"

Sure enough, a vast white cloud swam above them – but just near by was a hole right through the cloud!

"That's where we go, up that hole," said Jo. "See that branch that goes up the hole? Come on!"

They all went up the last and topmost branch of the Faraway Tree. It went up and up through the purple hole in the cloud. At the very end of the branch was a little ladder.

Jo climbed the ladder – and suddenly his head poked out into the Land of Topsy-Turvy!

Then one by one all the others followed – and soon all seven of them stood in the curious land.

Dick was not as used to strange lands as were

the others. He stood and stared, with his eyes so wide open that it really seemed as if they were going to drop out of his head!

And, indeed, it was a strange sight he saw. Every house was upside down, and stood on its chimneys. The trees were upside down, their heads buried in the ground and their roots in the air. And, dear me, the people walked upside-down, too!

"They are walking on their hands, with their legs in the air!" said Jo. "Goodness, what a queer thing to do!"

Everyone stared at the folk of Topsy-Turvy Land. They got along very quickly on their hands, and often stopped to talk to one another, chattering busily. Some of them had been shopping, and carried their baskets on one foot.

"Let's go and peep inside a house and see what it's like, all topsy-turvy," said Jo. So they set off to the nearest house. It looked most peculiar standing on its chimneys. No smoke came out of them—but smoke came out of a window near the top.

"How do we get in?" said Bessie. They watched a Topsy-Turvy man walk on his hands to another house. He jumped in at the nearest window, going up a ladder first.

The children looked for the ladder that entered the house they were near. They soon found it. They went up it to a window and peeped inside.

"Gracious!" said Jo. "Everything really *is* upside down in it—the chairs and tables, and everything. How uncomfortable it must be!"

An old lady was inside the house. She was sitting upside down in an upside-down chair and looked very peculiar. She was angry when she saw the children peeping in.

She clapped her hands, and a tall man, walking on his hands, came running in from the next room.

"Send those rude children away," shouted the old woman. The tall man hurried to the window on his hands, and the children quickly slid down the ladder, for the man looked rather fierce.

"It's a silly land, I think," said Jo. "I vote we just have our lunch and then leave this place. I wonder why everything is topsy-turvy."

"Oh, a spell was put on everything and everybody," said Moon-Face, "and in a trice everything was topsy-turvy. Look – wouldn't that be a good place to sit and eat our lunch in?"

It was under a big oak tree whose roots stood high in the air. Jo and Moon-Face set out the lunch. It looked very good.

"There's plenty for everybody," said Jo. "Have a sandwich, Silky?"

"Saucepan, have a plum?"

"Crumb?" said Saucepan, in surprise. "Is that all you can spare for me – a crumb?"

"PLUM, PLUM, PLUM!" said Moon-Face, pushing a ripe one into the Saucepan Man's hands.

"Oh, *plum*," said Saucepan. "Well, why didn't you say so?"

Everybody giggled. They all set to work to eat a good lunch.

In the middle of it, Jo happened to look round, and he saw something surprising.

It was a policeman coming along, walking on his hands, of course.

"Look what's coming," said Jo with a laugh. Everyone looked. Moon-Face went pale.

"I don't like the look of him," he said. "Suppose he's come to lock us up for something? We couldn't get away down the Faraway Tree before this land swung away from the top!"

The policeman came right up to the little crowd under the tree.

"Why aren't you Topsy-Turvy?" he asked in a stern voice. "Don't you know that the rule in this land is that everything and everyone has to be upside-down?"

"Yes, but we don't belong to this silly land," said Jo. "And if you were sensible, you'd make another rule, saying that everybody must be the right way up. You've just no idea how silly you look, policeman, walking on your hands!"

The policeman went red with anger. He took a sort of stick from his belt and tapped Jo on the head with it.

"Topsy-Turvy!" he said. "Topsy-Turvy!"

And to Jo's horror he had to turn himself upside-down at once! The others stared at poor Jo, standing on his hands, his legs in the air.

"Oh, golly!" cried Jo. "I can't eat anything properly now because I need my hands to walk with. Policeman, put me right again."

"You *are* right now," said the policeman, and walked solemnly away on his hands.

"Put Jo the right way up," said Dick. So everyone tried to get him over so that he was the right way up again. But as soon as they got his legs down and his head up, he turned topsy-turvy again. He just couldn't help it, for he was under a spell.

A group of Topsy-Turvy people came to watch. They laughed loudly. "Now he belongs to Topsy-Turvy Land!" they cried. "He'll have to stay here with us. Never mind, boy – you'll soon get used to it!"

"Take me back to the Faraway Tree," begged Jo, afraid that he really and truly *might* be made to stay in this queer land. "Hurry!"

Everyone jumped to their feet. They helped Jo along to where the hole ran down through the cloud. He wasn't used to walking on his hands and he kept falling over. They tried their best to make him stand upright, but he couldn't. The spell wouldn't let him.

"It will be difficult to get him down through the hole," said Dick. "Look—there it is. I'd better go down first and see if I can help him. You others push him through as carefully as you can. He'll have to go upside down, I'm afraid."

It was very difficult to get Jo through the hole, because his hands and head had to go first. Moon-Face held his legs to guide him. Dick held his shoulders as he came down the ladder, so that he wouldn't fall.

At last they were all seven through the hole in the clouds, and were on the broad branch outside Moon-Face's house. Jo held on to the branch with his hands, his legs were in the air.

"Moon-Face! Silky! Can't you possibly take this spell away?" groaned he. "It's dreadful."

"Silky, what land is coming to the top of the Faraway Tree next?" asked Moon-Face. "Have you heard?"

"I think it's the Land of Spells," said Silky. "It should come to-morrow. But I'm not really sure."

"Oh, well, if it's the Land of Spells, we could easily get a spell from there to put Jo right," said Moon-Face, beaming. "Jo, you must stay the night with me and wait for the Land of Spells tomorrow. The others can go home and tell what has happened."

"All right," said Jo. "I can't possibly climb up the tree again if I'm upside down – so I'll just have to wait here. Mother will never believe it, though, when the others tell her why I don't go home. Still, it can't be helped."

They all went into Moon-Face's house. Jo stood on a chair, upside down. The others sat about and talked. Dick was sorry for Jo, but he couldn't help feeling a bit excited. Goodness – if this was the sort of adventure that Jo, Bessie and Fanny had, what fun things were going to be!

The others began telling him all the adventures they had had. Silky made some tea, and went down the tree to fetch some more Pop Biscuits. When it was half-past five Bessie said they must go.

"Good-bye, Jo," she said. "Don't be too unhappy. Pretend you are a bat – they always sleep upside down, you know, and don't mind a bit! Come on, Dick – we're going down the slippery-slip!"

Dick *was* excited. He took the red cushion that Moon-Face gave him and sat himself at the top of the slide. Bessie gave him a push.

And off he went, round and round the inside of the enormous Faraway Tree, sitting safely on his cushion. *What* a way to get down a tree!

IV

THE LAND OF SPELLS

Dick shot round down the inside of the Faraway Tree on his cushion. He came to the bottom. He shot out of the trap-door there, and landed on the soft green moss. He sat there for a moment, out of breath.

"That's the loveliest slide I've ever had!" he thought to himself. "O-o-oh – wouldn't I like to do that again!"

He had just got up from the moss when the trap-door at the bottom of the tree opened once again, and Fanny shot out on a yellow cushion. Then came Bessie, giggling, for she always thought it was a huge joke to slide down inside the tree like that.

"What do we do with the cushions?" asked Dick. "Does Moon-Face want them back?"

"Yes, he does," said Fanny, picking them up. "The red squirrel always collects them and sends them back to him."

As she spoke, a red squirrel, dressed in a jersey, popped out of a hole in the trunk.

"Here are the cushions," said Fanny, and the squirrel took them. He looked up into the tree, and a rope came swinging down.

"Moon-Face always lets it down for his cushions," said Bessie. Dick watched the squirrel tie the three cushions to the rope end. Then he gave three gentle tugs at the rope, and at once the rope was pulled up, and the cushions went swinging up the tree to Moon-Face.

"I wish Jo was with us," said Dick, as they all went home. "Do you suppose Aunt Polly will be worried about him?"

"Well, we'll have to tell Mother," said Fanny. "She is sure to ask where he is."

Mother did ask, of course, and the girls told her what had happened.

"I find all this very difficult to believe," said Mother, astonished. "I think Jo is just spending the night with Moon-Face for a treat. Well, he certainly must come back to-morrow, for there is work for him to do."

Nobody said any more. The girls and Dick felt very tired, and after some hot cocoa and potatoes cooked in their jackets for supper, they all went to bed. Bessie wondered how Jo was getting on at Moon-Face's.

He was getting on all right, though he was very tired of being upside down. It didn't matter how hard he tried to get the right way up, he always swung back topsy-turvy again. The policeman had put a very strong spell on him!

"You had better try to sleep in my bed," said Moon-Face. "I'll sleep on my sofa."

"I suppose I'll have to stand on my head all night," said poor Jo. And that's just what he did have to do. It was most uncomfortable.

Once he lost his balance when he was asleep, and tipped off the bed. He almost fell down the slippery-slip, but Moon-Face, who was awake, reached out a hand and caught his leg just in time.

"Gracious!" said Moon-Face. "Don't go doing things like this in the middle of the night, Jo. It's most upsetting."

"Well, how can I help it?" said Jo.

"I'll tie your feet to a nail on my wall," said Moon-Face. "Then you can't topple over when you are asleep."

So he did that, and Jo didn't fall down any more. When morning came he was most astonished to find himself upside-down, for at first he didn't remember what had happened.

"I'll just peep up through the hole in the cloud and see if by any chance the Land of Spells is there yet," said Moon-Face. "If it is, we'll go up and see what we can do for you."

So off he went up the little ladder and popped his head out of the hole in the cloud to see if the Land of Topsy-Turvy was still there, or if it had gone.

There was nothing there at all—only just the big white cloud, moving about like a thick mist. Moon-Face slipped down the ladder again.

"Topsy-Turvy has gone, but the next land hasn't come yet," he said. "We'll have breakfast and then I'll look again. Hallo—here's Silky. Stay and have breakfast, Silky darling."

"I came up to see how Jo was," said Silky. "Yes, I'd love to have breakfast. It's funny to watch Jo eating upside down. Hasn't the Land of Spells come yet?"

"Not yet," said Moon-Face, putting a kettle on

his stove to boil. "There's nothing there at all. But Topsy-Turvy is gone, thank goodness!"

They all had breakfast. Moon-Face cooked some porridge. "What do you want on your porridge?" he asked Jo. "Treacle – sugar – cream?"

Jo couldn't see any treacle, sugar or cream on the table. "Treacle," he said, "please, Moon-Face." Moon-Face handed him a small jug that seemed to be quite empty.

"Treacle!" he said to the jug in a firm voice. And treacle came pouring out as soon as Jo tipped up the jug. Silky wanted cream – and cream came out when Moon-Face said "Cream!" to the jug. It was great fun.

Moon-Face went again to see if the Land of Spells had come. This time he came back excited.

"It's there!" he said. "Come on! I'd better take some money with me, I think, in case we have to buy the spell we want."

He took a big purse down from a shelf, and then he and Silky helped Jo to walk upside down up the branch that led through the hole in the cloud to the little ladder. Up he went with great difficulty, holding on tightly to the rungs of the ladder with his hands. At last he was up in the Land of Spells.

This land was like a big market-place. In it were all kinds of curious little shops and stalls. All kinds of people sold spells. In some of the shops sat tall wizards, famous for magic. In some of them were green-eyed witches, making spells as fast as they could. Outside, in the market-place, sat all kinds of fairy folk at their stalls –

pixies, gnomes, goblins, elves—all crying their wares at the tops of their high voices.

"Spell to make a crooked nose straight!" cried one pixie, rattling a yellow box in which were magic pills.

"Spell to grow blue daffodils!" cried a gnome, showing a bottle of blue juice.

"Spell to make cats sing!" cried another gnome. Jo could hardly believe his ears. How queer! Who would want to make cats sing?

"Now, we must just see if we can possibly find a spell to make you stand up straight again," said Moon-Face, and he went into a little low shop in which sat a strange goblin.

The goblin had blue, pointed ears, and his eyes sparkled as if they had fireworks in them.

"I want a spell," said Moon-Face.

"What for?" asked the goblin. "I've a spell for everything under the sun in my shop! Very powerful spells too, some of them. Would you like a spell to send you travelling straight off to the moon?"

"Oh, no, thank you," said Moon-Face at once. "I know I look like the man in the moon, with my big round face—but I'm nothing at all to do with the moon really."

"Well, would you like a spell to make you as tall as a giant?" said the goblin, picking up a box and opening it. He showed Moon-Face a large blue pill inside. "Now, take that pill, and you'll shoot up as high as a house! You'll feel fine. It only costs one piece of gold."

"No, thank you," said Moon-Face. "If I grew as big as that I'd never get down the hole in the cloud back to the Faraway Tree. And if I did, I'd never be able to get in at the door of my tree-house. I don't want silly spells like that."

"Silly!" cried the goblin, in a rage. "You call my marvellous spells silly! Another word from you, stupid old Round-Face, and I'll use a spell that will turn you into a big bouncing ball!"

Silky pulled Moon-Face out of the shop quickly. She was quite white. "Moon-Face, you know you shouldn't make these people cross," she whispered. "Why, you may find yourself nothing but a bouncing ball, or a black beetle, or something, if you are rude to them. For goodness' sake, let *me* ask for the spell we want. Look – here's a bigger shop – with a nice-looking witch inside."

They all went in. The witch was knitting stockings from the green smoke that came from her fire. It was marvellous to watch her. Jo wished he wasn't upside-down so that he might see her properly.

"Good morning," said the witch. "Do you want a spell?"

"Yes, please," said Silky in her most polite voice. "We want to make our friend Jo come the right way up again."

"That's easy," said the witch, her green eyes looking in a kindly way at poor Jo. "I've only got to rub a Walking-Spell on to the soles of his feet – and he will be all right. The Walking-Spell will make his feet want to walk – and he will have to stand up the right way to walk on them—so he will be cured. Come here, boy!"

Jo walked over to the witch on his hands. She took down a jar from a shelf and opened it. It was full of purple ointment. The witch rubbed some on to the soles of Jo's shoes.

"Rimminy-Romminy-Reet,
Stand on your own two feet!
Rimminy-Romminy-Ro,
The right way up you must go!"

And, of course, you can guess what happened! Jo swung right over, stood on his two feet again, and there he was, as upright as Moon-Face and Silky. Wasn't he glad!

V

SAUCEPAN MAKES A MUDDLE

Jo, Silky and Moon-Face were so very pleased that Jo was the right way up again.

"It feels funny," said Jo. "I feel quite giddy the right way up after standing upside-down for so long. Thank you, witch. How much is the spell?"

"One piece of gold," said the witch. Moon-Face put his hand into his large purse. He brought out a piece of gold. The witch threw it into the fire, and at once bright golden smoke came out. She took up her knitting-needles and began to knit the yellow smoke into the stockings she was making.

"I wanted a yellow pattern," she said, pleased. "Your piece of gold came just at the right moment."

"Golly, this is a very magic land, isn't it?" said Jo, as the three of them walked out of the queer shop. "Fancy knitting stockings out of smoke! Don't let's go home yet, Moon-Face. I want to see a few more things."

"All right," said Moon-Face, who wanted to explore a bit, too. "Come on. I say, look at the gnome who is selling a spell to make cats sing! Somebody has brought his cat to him – I wonder if the spell will really work!"

The servant of a witch had brought along a big black cat. He handed the gnome two silver pieces of money. The gnome took the cat on his knee. He opened its mouth and looked down it. Then he took a silver whistle and blew a tune softly down the cat's pink throat. The cat swallowed once or twice and then jumped off the gnome's knee.

"Will it sing now?" asked the witch's servant. "I daren't go back to my mistress unless it does."

"It will sing whenever you pull its tail," said the gnome, turning to another customer.

The witch's servant went off with the cat following behind. Jo took hold of Moon-Face's arm and whispered to him:

"I'm going to pull the cat's tail. I do SO want to hear if it really will sing!"

Moon-Face and Silky wanted to as well. They giggled to see Jo running softly after the big black cat. He took hold of its tail. He gave it a gentle pull.

And then, oh, what a peculiar thing! The cat stopped, lifted up its head, and sang in a very deep man's voice:

"Oh, once my whiskers grew so long
I had to have a shave!
The barber said: 'It's not the way
For whiskers to behave,
If you're not careful, my dear cat,
They'll grow into a beard,
And then a billy-goat you'll be,
Or something very weird!'

"Oh, once my tail became so short
It hadn't got a wag,
The grocer said . . ."

But what the grocer said about the cat's short tail nobody ever knew. The servant of the witch turned round in surprise when he heard the cat singing, for he knew that he hadn't pulled the cat's tail. He saw Jo and the others grinning away near by, and he was very angry.

"How dare you use up the cat's singing!" he cried. "You wait till I tell the witch. She'll be after you. And *you* won't sing if she catches you!"

"Quick! Run!" said Moon-Face. "If he does fetch the witch we'll get into trouble."

So they ran away fast, and were soon out of

sight of the cat and the servant. They sank down under a tree, laughing.

"Oh, dear! That cat did sing a funny song!" said Jo, wiping his eyes. "And what a lovely deep voice it had. Do you suppose its whiskers really did grow very long?"

Just then the three heard a loud noise coming along: "Clankily-clank, rattle, bang, crash!"

"The Saucepan Man!" they all cried. "He's come up here, too!"

And sure enough, it *was* old Saucepan, grinning all over his funny face. He had so many kettles and saucepans on that day that nothing could be seen of him except his face and his feet.

"Hallo, hallo!" he said. "I guessed you were up here. Been having fun?"

"Yes," said Jo. "I'm all right again – look! It's so nice to walk the proper way up again. And oh, Saucepan, we've just heard a cat sing!"

Saucepan actually heard what Joe said – but he couldn't believe that he had heard right, so he put his hand behind his ear and said, "What did you say? I thought you said you'd heard a cat sing – but I heard wrong, I know."

"No, you heard right," said Moon-Face. "We *did* hear a cat sing!"

"Let's go and explore a bit more," said Jo. So up they got and off they went.

A witch was selling a spell to make ordinary broomsticks fly through the air. The four watched in amazement as they saw her rubbing a pink ointment on to a broomhandle belonging to an elf.

"Now get on it, say 'Whizz away!' and you can fly home," said the witch. The elf got astride the broomstick, a smile on her pretty face.

"Whizz away!" she said. And off whizzed the broomstick up into the air, with the elf clinging tightly to it!

"I'd like to buy that spell," said Jo. "I wonder how much it is."

The witch heard him. "Three silver pieces," she said. Jo hadn't even got one. But Moon-Face had. He took them out of his large purse and gave them to the witch.

"Where's your broomstick?" she said.

"We haven't got one with us," said Jo. "But can't you give us the ointment instead, please?"

"Well, I'll give you just a little," said the witch. She took a tiny pink jar and put a dab of the pink ointment into it. Jo took it and put it into his pocket. Now maybe his mother's broomstick would learn to fly!

At the next stall a goblin was selling a spell to make things big. The spell was in big tins, and looked like paint.

"Just think what a useful spell this is!" yelled the goblin to the passers-by. "Have you visitors coming to tea and only a small cake to offer them? A dab of this spell and the cake swells to twice its size! Have you a suit you have grown out of' A dab of this spell and it will grow to the right size! Marvellous, wonderful, amazing and astonishing! Buy, buy, buy, whilst you've got the chance!"

Saucepan heard all that the goblin said, for he was shouting at the top of his voice. He began to look in all his kettles and saucepans.

"What do you want?" asked Jo.

"My money," said the Saucepan Man. "I always keep it in one of my kettles or saucepans – but I never remember which. I simply *must* buy that spell. Think how useful it would be to me. Sometimes when I go round selling my goods a customer will say to me, 'Oh, you haven't a big enough kettle!' But now I shall be able to make my kettles just as big as I like! And we can dab the Pop Biscuits with the spell, too, and make them twice as big."

He found his money at last and paid it to the

goblin, who handed him a tin of the spell. Saucepan was very pleased. He longed to try it on something. He took the brush and dabbed a daisy nearby with the spell. The daisy at once grew to twice its size. Then Saucepan dabbed a bumble-bee and that grew enormous. It buzzed around Moon-Face and he waved it away.

"Saucepan, don't do any more bees," he begged. "I expect their stings are twice as big, too. Look – let's go to that sweet-shop over there and buy some sweets. It would be fun to make them twice as big!"

They hurried to the shop – but on the way a dreadful thing happened! Saucepan fell over one of his kettles and upset the tin in which he carried the spell. It splashed up – and drops of it fell on to Moon-Face, Silky, Jo – and the old Saucepan Man, too! And in a trice they all shot up to twice their size! Silky grew to three times her size because more drops fell on her.

They stared at one another. How small the Land of Spells suddenly seemed! How little the witches and goblins looked, how tiny the shops were!

"Saucepan! You really *are* careless!" cried Moon-Face, vexed. "Look what you've done to us. *Now* what are we to do?"

Silky clutched hold of Moon-Face's arm. "Moon-Face!" she said. "Oh, Moon-Face – do you suppose we are too big to go down the hole through the cloud?"

Moon-Face turned pale. "We'd better go and

see," he said. "Come on, everybody."

Frightened and silent, all four of them hurried to where the hole led down to the Faraway Tree. How little it seemed to the four big people now! Moon-Face tried to get down. He stuck. He couldn't slip down at all.

"It's no use," he said. "We're too big to go down. Whatever in the world shall we do?"

VI

WHAT CAN THEY DO NOW?

Jo, Moon-Face, Silky and Saucepan sat down by the hole and thought hard. Silky began to cry.

The Saucepan Man looked most uncomfortable. He was very fond of Silky. "Silky, please do forgive me for being so careless," he said in a small voice. "I didn't mean to do this. Don't cry. You make me feel dreadful."

"It's all right," sobbed Silky, borrowing Moon-Face's hanky. "I know you didn't mean to. But I can't help feeling dreadfully sad when I think I won't ever be able to see my dear little room in the Faraway Tree any more."

The Saucepan Man began to cry, too. Tears dripped with a splash into his saucepans and kettles. He put his arm round Silky, and two or three kettle-spouts stuck into her.

"Don't!" she said. "You're sticking into me. Moon-Face – Jo – can't you think of something to do? Can we possibly squeeze down if we hold our breaths and make ourselves as small as we can?"

"Quite impossible," said Moon-Face gloomily. "Listen – there's somebody coming up the ladder."

They heard voices – and soon a head popped up out of the hole in the cloud. It was Dick's! He stared in the very greatest surprise at the four enormous people sitting by the hole.

He climbed up and stood beside them, looking very, very small. Then up came Bessie and Fanny. Their eyes nearly fell out of their heads when they saw how big Jo and his friends were.

"What's happened?" cried Dick. "We began to be worried because you didn't come home, Jo – so we climbed up to see where you were. But why are you so ENORMOUS?"

Jo told them. Silky sobbed into Moon-Face's hanky. Bessie put her arm round her. It was funny to feel Silky so very big. Bessie's arm only went half round Silky's waist!

"And now, you see, we can't get back down the hole," said Jo.

"*I* know what you can do!" said Dick suddenly.

"What?" cried everyone hopefully.

"Why, rub the hole with the spell, and it will get bigger, of course!" said Dick. "Then you'll be able to get down it."

"Why ever didn't we think of that before!" cried Jo, jumping up. "Saucepan, where's that tin with the spell in?"

He picked up the tin—but, alas! it was quite, quite empty. Every single drop had been spilt when Saucepan had fallen over.

"Well, never mind!" said Moon-Face, cheering up. "We can go and buy some more from that goblin. Come on!"

They all set off, Dick, Bessie and Fanny looking very small indeed by the others. They went up to the goblin who had sold them the spell.

"May we have another tin of that spell you sold us just now?" asked Moon-Face, holding out the empty tin.

"I've not the tiniest drop left," said the goblin. "And I can't make any more till the full moon comes. It can only be made in the moonlight."

Everyone looked so miserable that the goblin felt sorry for them. "Why do you look so unhappy?" he said. "What has happened?"

Jo told him everything. The goblin listened with great interest. Then he smiled. "Well, my dear boy," he said, "if you can't get a spell to make the hole big, why don't you buy a spell to make yourselves small? My brother, the green goblin over there, sells that kind of spell. Only be careful not to put too much on yourselves, or you may go smaller than you mean to!"

They went over to the green goblin. He was yelling at the top of his voice.

"Buy my wonderful and most amazing spell! It will make anything as small as you like! Have you an enemy? Dab him with this and see him shrink to the size of a mouse! Have you too big a nose? Dab it with this and make it the right size! Oh, wonderful, astonishing, amazing. . . ."

Everyone hurried up. Moon-Face took some money out of his purse. "I'll have the spell, please," he said. The green goblin gave him a tin. The spell in it looked rather like paint, just as the other had done.

"Now go slow," said the goblin. "You don't want to get too small. Try a little at a time."

Moon-Face dabbed a little on Silky. She went a bit smaller at once. He dabbed again. She went smaller still.

"Is she the right size yet?" asked Moon-Face. Everyone stared at Silky.

"Not *quite*," said Bessie. "But she is almost, Moon-Face. So be careful with your next dab."

Moon-Face was very careful. At the next dab of the spell Silky went to exactly her right size. She was so pleased.

"Now you, Jo," said Moon-Face. So he dabbed Jo and got Jo back to his right size again, too. Then he tried dabbing the Saucepan Man, and soon got him right. His kettles and saucepans went right, too. It was funny to watch them.

"Now I'll do you, Moon-Face," said Jo.

"No, thanks, I'll do myself," said Moon-Face. He dabbed the spell on to himself and shrank smaller. He dabbed again and went smaller still. Then he stopped dabbing and put the brush down.

"You're not quite your ordinary size yet," said Jo.

"I know," said Moon-Face. "But I always thought I was a bit on the short side. Now I'm just about right. I always wanted to be a bit taller. I shan't dab myself any more."

Everyone laughed. It was funny to see Moon-Face a bit taller than usual. As they stood there and laughed, a curious cold wind began to blow. Moon-Face looked all round and then began to shout.

"Quick, quick! The Land of Spells is on the move! Hurry before we get left behind!"

Everyone got a shock. Good gracious! It would never do to be left behind, just as everyone had got small enough to go down the hole in the clouds.

They set off to the hole. The wind blew more and more strongly, and suddenly the sun went out. It was almost as if somebody had blown it out, Jo thought. At once darkness fell on the Land of Spells.

"Take hold of hands, take hold of hands!" cried Jo. "We shall lose one another if we don't!"

They all took hold of one another's hands and called out their names to make sure everyone was there. They stumbled on through the darkness.

"Here's the hole!" cried Jo, at last, and down he went. He felt the ladder and climbed down that, too. The others followed one by one, pushing close behind in the dark, longing to get down to the Faraway Tree they knew so well. How lovely it would be to sit in Moon-Face's room and feel safe!

But down at the bottom of the ladder there was no Faraway Tree. Instead, to Jo's astonishment, there was a narrow passage, lit by a swinging green lantern.

"I say," he said to the others, "What's this? Where's the Faraway Tree?"

"We've come down the wrong hole," groaned Moon-Face. "Oh, goodness, what bad luck!"

"Well, where are we?" asked Dick in wonder.

"I don't know," said Moon-Face. "We'd better follow this passage and see where it leads to. It's no use climbing back and trying to find the right hole. We'd never find it in the dark—and anyway, I'm pretty sure the Land of Spells has moved on by now."

Everyone felt very gloomy. Jo led the way down the passage. It twisted and turned, went up and down steps, and was lighted here and there by the green lanterns swinging from the roof.

At last they came to a big yellow door. On it was a blue knocker, a blue bell, a blue letter-box and a blue notice that said:

"Mister Change-About. Knock once, ring twice, and rattle the letter-box."

Jo knocked once, very loudly. Then he rang twice, and everyone heard the bell going "R-r-r-r-r-ring! R-r-r-r-r-ring!" Then he rattled the letter-box.

The door didn't open. It completely disappeared. It was most peculiar. One minute it was there—and the next it had gone, and there was nothing in front of them. They could see right into a big underground room.

At the end of it, by a roaring fire, a round fat person was sitting. "That must be Mister Change-About!" whispered Dick. "Dare we go in?"

VII

MR. CHANGE-ABOUT AND THE ENCHANTER

Everyone stared at Mr. Change-About. At least, as he was the only person in the room, they thought that was who it must be. He got up and came towards them.

He was a fat, comfortable-looking person with a broad smile on his face. "Dear me, what a lot of visitors!" he said. "Do sit down."

There was nowhere to sit except the floor. This was made of stone and looked rather cold. So nobody sat down.

Something happened to Mr. Change-About when nobody obeyed him. He grew tall and thin. His broad smile disappeared and a frown came all over his face. He looked a most unpleasant person.

"SIT DOWN!" he roared. And everybody sat down in a hurry!

Mr. Change-About looked at the Saucepan Man, who had sat down with a tremendous clatter.

"Have you a nice little kettle that would boil enough water for two cups of tea?" he asked.

The Saucepan Man didn't hear. So Jo shouted

in his ear, and he beamed, got up, and undid a little kettle from the many that hung about him.

"Just the thing!" he said, handing it to Mr. Change-About. "Try it and see!"

Mr. Change-About changed again, and became a happy-looking little creature with dancing eyes and a sweet smile. He took the kettle.

"Thank you," he said. "So kind of you. Just what I wanted. How much is it?"

"Nothing at all," said the Saucepan Man. "Just a present to you!"

"Well, allow me to hand round some chocolate to you all in return for such a nice present," said Mr. Change-About, and fetched an enormous box of chocolates from a cupboard. Everybody was pleased.

Dick looked carefully into the box when his turn came. His hand stretched out for the very biggest chocolate of all. Mr. Change-About at once changed again and flew into a rage.

He became thin and mean-looking, his nose shot out long, and his eyes grew small.

"Bad boy, greedy boy!" he shouted. "You shan't any of you have my chocolates now! Horrid, greedy children!"

And at once all the chocolates changed to little hard stones. Bessie had hers in her mouth, and she spat it out at once. The others looked most disgusted. The old Saucepan Man gave a yell of dismay.

"I've swallowed mine—and now I suppose I've got a stone inside me. Oh, you nasty Mr. Change-About! I'll show you what I think of your chocolates!"

And to everyone's surprise Saucepan rushed at Mr. Change-About, knocked his box of chocolates all over the room, and began to pummel him hard.

Biff, smack, biff, smack! Goodness, how the old Saucepan Man fought Mr. Change-About. And Mr. Change-About fought back—but what was the good of that? Saucepan was so hung about with pans of all kinds that nobody could possibly hit him anywhere without grazing their knuckles and hurting themselves very much indeed!

Clang, clatter, clang, clatter, clash! The kettles and saucepans made an enormous noise, and everyone began to laugh, for really Saucepan looked too funny for words, dancing about on the floor, hitting and slapping at Mr. Change-About.

Mr. Change-About suddenly got very big and fierce-looking, but old Saucepan didn't seem to mind at all. He just went on hitting out at him, and shouted: "The bigger you are, the more there is to hit!"

So then Mr. Change-About got very small indeed, as small as a mouse, and ran squealing across the floor in fright. Quick as lightning, Saucepan picked him up, popped him into a kettle, and put the lid on him!

"Oh, Saucepan! Whatever will you do next?" said Jo, wiping tears of laughter from his eyes. "I've never seen such a funny fight in my life. Be careful Mr. Change-About doesn't squeeze out of the spout."

"I'll stuff it with paper," said Saucepan, tearing some from the box of chocolates. "Now he's safe. Well – what do we do next?"

"We'd better get out of here," said Jo, standing up. He turned towards the doorway – but what was this! There was no doorway – and no door! Only a wall of rock that ran all round the underground room now.

"Goodness! How *do* we get out?" said Jo, puzzled. "This is a very magic kind of place."

"There's no window, of course, because we are underground," said Dick. "What in the wide world are we going to do?"

"What about the chimney?" asked Fanny, running to the fire. "It looks pretty big. We could put the fire out and climb up, perhaps."

"Well, that looks about our only chance of getting out of here," said Jo. He looked round for some water to put out the fire. He saw a tap jutting out from the wall and went to it. He put a pail underneath and turned on the tap. The water was bright green, and soon filled the pail. Jo threw it on the fire. It made a terrific sizzling noise and went out at once, puffing clouds of green smoke into the room.

Jo stepped on to the dead fire and looked up the chimney. "There's an iron ladder going right up!" he called in excitement. "Come on! We shall get dirty, but we can't help that. Hurry, before anything else queer happens!"

Up the ladder he went. It was hot from the heat of the fire, but grew colder the higher he went.

"What an enormously long chimney!" called back Jo. "Is everyone coming?"

"Yes! Yes!" called six voices below him. Jo climbed steadily upwards. At last the ladder came to an end. Joe clambered over the top of it and found himself in a most peculiar place.

"This looks like some kind of cellar," he said to the others, as they scrambled up beside him. "Look at all those sacks piled up! What do you suppose is in them?"

"Let's look," said Dick, who was always curious about everything. He undid a sack–and, goodness gracious me!–out poured a great stream of bright golden pieces of money! Everyone looked at it in astonishment.

"Somebody VERY rich must live here," said

Jo at last. "I never in my life saw so much gold. I can't believe that *all* the sacks are full of it!"

He undid another sack–and out poured gold again. Just as everyone was running their fingers through it, marvelling at the gleam and shine of so much gold, there came the sound of quick footsteps overhead.

A door above them opened, and a gleam of sunlight shone on to a flight of stone steps leading up from the cellar to the door. A tall man in a pointed hat looked down.

"Golly! It's an enchanter!" whispered Moon-Face in a fright. "We must still be in the Land of Spells. Oh, dear!"

"Robbers! Thieves! Burglars!" shouted the enchanter in a loud voice. "Servants, come here! Capture these robbers! They are after my gold! See–they have undone two sacks already!"

"We don't want your gold!" cried Dick. "We only just wanted to know what was in all these sacks!"

"I don't believe you!" cried the enchanter, as about a dozen small imps came running past him down the steps into the cellar. "Capture them, servants, and tie them up!"

The little imps pulled everyone up the cellar steps into a big, sunlit room. Its ceiling was so high that nobody could see it. "Now tie them up," commanded the enchanter.

Moon-Face suddenly snatched a kettle from Saucepan and snapped the string that tied it to him. He went towards the enchanter fearlessly.

"Wait!" he cried, much to the astonishment of all the others. "Wait before you do this foolish thing! *I* am an enchanter, too—and in this kettle I have Mr. Change-About! Yes—he is a prisoner there! And let me tell you this, that if you dare to tie me up, I'll put *you* into the kettle, too, with Mr. Change-About!"

From the kettle came a small, squealing voice: "Set me free, Enchanter, set me free! Oh, do set me free!"

The enchanter turned quite pale. He knew it was Mr. Change-About's voice.

"Er—er—this is most peculiar," he said. "How did you capture Mr. Change-About? He is a very powerful person, and a great friend of mine."

"Oh, I'm not going to tell you what magic I used," said Moon-Face boldly. "Now—are you going to let us go—or shall I put you into this kettle, too?"

"I'll let you go," said the enchanter, and he waved them all towards a door at the end of the room. "You may leave at once."

Everyone rushed to the door gladly. They all ran through it, expecting to come out into the sunshine.

But, alas for them! The enchanter had played them a trick! They found themselves going up many hundreds of stairs, up and up and up—and when they came to the top there was nothing but a round room with one small window! A bench stood at one end and a table at the other.

The enchanter's voice floated up to them.

"Ho! ho! I've got you nicely! Now I'm going to get my friend, Wizard Wily, and he'll soon tell me how to deal with robbers like you!"

"We *are* in a trap!" groaned Jo. "Moon-Face, you were very clever and very brave. But honestly, we are worse off than ever. I simply don't see any way out of this at all!"

VIII

HOW CAN THEY ESCAPE?

Moon-Face looked all round the room at the top of the tower. "Well, we're in a nice fix now," he said gloomily. "It's no use going down the stairs again – we shall find the door at the bottom locked. And what's the good of a window that is half a mile from the ground!"

Jo looked out of the window. "Gracious!" he said, "the tower is awfully tall! I can hardly see the bottom of it. Hallo – there's the enchanter going off in his carriage. I suppose he is going to fetch his friend, dear Wizard Wily."

"I don't like the sound of Wizard Wily," said Silky. "Jo – Dick – Moon-Face – please, please think of some way to escape!"

But there just simply WASN'T any way. No one wanted to jump out of the window.

They all sat down. "I'm dreadfully hungry," said Bessie. "Has anyone got anything to eat?"

"I may have got some Pop Biscuits," said

Moon-Face, feeling in his pockets. But he hadn't. "Feel in *your* pockets, Jo and Dick."

Both boys felt, hoping to find a bit of toffee or half a biscuit. Dick brought out a collection of string, bits of paper, a pencil and a few marbles. Jo took out much the same kind of things – but with his rubbish came a pink jar, very small and heavy.

"What's in that jar?" asked Bessie, who hadn't seen it before. "Isn't it pretty?"

"Let me see – what can it be?" wondered Jo, as he unscrewed the lid. "Oh – I know. We saw a witch selling whizz-away ointment for broomsticks in the Land of Spells – and I thought it *would* be such fun to rub some on mother's broomstick and see it fly through the air. So we bought some. Smell it – it's delicious."

Everyone smelt it. Moon-Face suddenly got tremendously excited. "I say——" he began. "I say – oh, I say!"

"Well, say then!" said Jo. "What's the matter?"

"Oh, I SAY!" said Moon-Face, stammering all the more. "Listen! If only we could get a broomstick – we could rub this pink ointment on it – and fly away on it!"

"Moon-Face, that's a very good idea – if only we had a broomstick – but we haven't!" said Jo. "Look at this room – a table and a bench – no sign of a broomstick at all!"

"Well, I'll run down the stairs and see if I can possibly get a broomstick," said Moon-Face, getting all excited. "I saw some standing in a corner of that room we were in. I'll do my best, anyway!"

"Good old Moon-Face!" said everyone, as they watched the round-faced little fellow scurry down the hundreds of steps. "If only he gets a broomstick!"

Moon-Face hurried down and down. It did seem such a very long way. At last he came to the bottom of the stairs. An enormous wooden door was at the bottom, fast shut. Moon-Face tried to open it, but he couldn't. So he banged on the door loudly.

A surprised voice called out: "Hie, there! What are you banging on the door for? What do you want?"

"A broomstick!" said Moon-Face loudly.

"A *broom*stick!" said the voice, more astonished than ever. "Whatever for?"

"To sweep up some crumbs!" said Moon-Face, quite untruthfully.

"A dust-pan and brush will do for that!" cried the voice, and the door opened a crack. A dust-pan and brush shot in with a clatter and came to rest by Moon-Face's feet. Then the door shut with a bang and was bolted at the other side.

"A dust-pan and brush!" said Moon-Face in disgust. "Now, who can ride away on those?" He banged on the door again.

"*Now* what's the matter?" yelled the voice angrily.

"These won't do," said Moon-Face. "I want a BROOMSTICK!"

"Well, go on wanting," said the voice. "You won't get one. I suppose you think you'll fly away on one if I give it to you. I'm not quite so silly as that. What do you suppose my master would say to me when he came back if I'd given you one of his broomsticks to escape on?"

Moon-Face groaned. He knew it was no good asking again. He picked up the dust-pan and brush and climbed the stairs slowly, suddenly feeling very tired.

Everyone was waiting for him. "Did you get it, Moon-Face?" they cried. But when they saw Moon-Face's gloomy face and the dust-pan and brush in his hand, they were very sad.

They all sat down to think. Jo looked up. "I suppose it wouldn't be any good rubbing the whizz-away ointment on to anything else?" he asked. "Would it make anything but broomsticks fly away?"

"I shouldn't think so," said Moon-Face. "But we could try. What is there to try on, though? We haven't a stick of any sort."

"No—but there's a table over there, and this bench," said Jo, getting excited. "Couldn't we try on those? We could easily sit on them and fly off, if only the magic would work."

"But it won't," said Silky. "I'm sure of that. It's only for broomsticks. But try it, Jo."

Jo took off the lid of the jar again. He dabbed a finger into the pink ointment and rubbed some all over the top of the wooden bench, which was very like a form at school. "Now for the table," said

Jo. He turned it upside down, thinking that it would be more comfortable to sit on that way. They could hold the legs as they went!

He rubbed the ointment all over the underside of the table. As he was doing this everyone heard the sound of horses' hoofs clip-clopping outside. Silky ran to the window.

"It's the enchanter come back again – and he's got the Wizard Wily with him!" she cried. "Oh, do be quick, Jo! They will be up here in a minute."

"Moon-Face, Silky and Saucepan, you sit on the bench," said Jo. "You girls and Dick and I will sit on the table. Hurry now!"

Everyone scrambled to take their seats. Silky was trembling with excitement. She could hear the footsteps of the enchanter and the wizard coming up the steps.

"Now, hold tight, in case we really do go off!" said Joe. "Ready, everyone? Then WHIZZ-AWAY HOME!"

And, goodness gracious, the bench and the table began to move! Yes, they really did! They moved slowly at first, for they were not used to whizzing away – but as the children squealed and squeaked in surprise and delight, the table rose up suddenly to the window and tried to get out!

It stuck. It couldn't get through. "Oh, table, do your best!" cried Jo. "The enchanter is nearly here!"

The table tipped itself up a little – and then it could just manage to squeeze through the opening. The children each clung tightly to a leg, afraid of being tipped off. Then at last the table was through the window, and, sailing away upside down, its four legs in the air, carrying the excited children safely, it whizzed off over the Land of Spells!

Jo looked back to see if the wooden bench was coming, too. It had had to wait until the table was through the window. Just as it was about to jerk upwards to the window, the enchanter and the Wizard Wily had come rushing into the room. What would have happened if the old Saucepan Man hadn't suddenly thrown a kettle at them, goodness knows!

It was the kettle with Mr. Change-About in! The lid came off. Mr. Change-About jumped out and turned himself almost into a giant! The enchanter fell over him, and Mr. Change-About, not seeing who it was at all, began to pummel him hard with his big fists, crying: "I'll teach you to put me into a kettle!"

Wily hit out at Mr. Change-About, not knowing in the least who he was, or where he had suddenly sprung from. And there was a perfectly marvellous fight going on, just as the wooden bench flew out of the window. The enchanter saw it going and tried to get hold of it—but just at that moment Mr. Change-About gave him such a hard punch on the nose that he fell over, smack, again!

"Go it, Change-About!" yelled Moon-Face. "Hit him hard!"

And out of the window sailed the bench, with

Moon-Face, Silky and Saucepan clinging tightly to it. Far away in the distance was the upside-down table.

The table whizzed steadily onwards, over hills and woods, and once over the sea. "We've come a very long way from home since we've been in the Land of Spells," said Jo. "I hope the table knows its way to our home. I don't want to land in any more strange lands just at present!"

The table knew its way all right. Jo gave a shout as it flew over a big dark wood. "The Enchanted Wood!" he cried. "We're nearly home!"

The table flew down to the garden of the children's cottage. Their mother was there, hanging out some clothes. She looked round in the greatest astonishment when she saw them arrive in such a peculiar way.

"Well, really!" she said. "Whatever next! Do you usually fly around the country in an upside-down table?"

"Oh, mother! We've had such an adventure!" said Jo, scrambling off. He looked up in the air to see if the bench was following – but there was no sign of it.

"Where's the bench?" said Dick. "Oh – I suppose it will go to the Faraway, as that is where the others live. Gracious – I feel all trembly. Jo – I am NOT going into any more lands at the top of the Faraway Tree again. It's just a bit too exciting!"

"Right," said Jo. "I feel the same. No more adventures for *me*!"

IX

THE LAND OF DREAMS

The children had had enough of adventures for some time. Their mother set them to work in the garden, and they did their best for her. Nobody suggested going to the Enchanted Wood at all.

"I hope old Moon-Face, Silky and the Saucepan Man got back to the tree safely," said Jo one day.

Moon-Face was wondering the same thing about the children. He and Silky talked about it.

"We haven't seen the children for ages," he said. "Let's slip down the tree, Silky, and make sure they got back all right, shall we? After all, it would be dreadful if they hadn't got back, and their mother was worrying about them."

So one afternoon, just after lunch, Silky and Moon-Face walked up to the door of the cottage. Bessie opened it and squealed with delight.

"Moon-Face! So you got back safely after all! Come in! Come in, Silky darling. Saucepan, you'll have to take off a kettle or two if you want to get in at the door."

The children's parents were out. The children and their friends sat and talked about their last adventure.

"What land is at the top of the tree now?" asked Dick curiously.

"Don't know," said Moon-Face. "Like to come and see?"

"No, thanks," said Jo at once. "We're not going up there any more."

"Well, come back and have tea with us," said Moon-Face. "Silky's got some Pop Biscuits – and I've made some Google Buns. I don't often make them – and I tell you they're a treat!"

"Google Buns!" said Bessie in astonishment. "Whatever are they?"

"You come and see," said Moon-Face, grinning. "They're better than Pop Biscuits – aren't they, Silky?"

"Much," said Silky.

"Well – Fanny and I have finished our work," said Bessie. "What about you boys?"

"We've got about half an hour's more work to do, that's all," said Jo. "If everyone helps, it will only take about ten minutes. We could leave a note for Mother. I would rather like to try those Google Buns!"

Well, everyone went into the garden to dig up the carrots and put them into piles. It didn't take more than ten minutes because they all worked so hard. They put away their tools, washed their hands, left a note for Mother – and then set off for the Enchanted Wood.

The Saucepan Man sang one of his ridiculous songs on the way:

> "Two tails for a kitten,
> Two clouds for the sky,
> Two pigeons for Christmas
> To make a plum pie!"

Everyone laughed. Jo, Bessie and Fanny had heard the Saucepan Man's silly songs before, but Dick hadn't.

"Go on," said Dick. "This is the silliest song I've ever heard."

The Saucepan Man clashed two kettles together as he sang:

> "Two roses for Bessie,
> Two spankings for Jo,
> Two ribbons for Fanny,
> With a ho-derry-ho!"

"It's an easy song to make up as you go along," said Bessie, giggling. "Every line but the last has to begin with the word 'Two'. Just think of any nonsense you like, and the song simply makes itself."

Singing silly songs, they all reached the Faraway Tree. Saucepan yelled up it: "Hie, Watzisname! Let down a rope, there's a good fellow! It's too hot to walk up to-day."

The rope came down. They all went up one by one, pulled high by the strong arms of Mister Watzisname.

Fanny was unlucky. She got splashed by Dame Washalot's water on the way up. "Next time I go up on the rope I shall take an umbrella with me," she said crossly.

"Come on," said Moon-Face. "Come and eat a Google Bun and see what you think of it."

Soon they were all sitting on the broad branches

outside Moon-Face's house, eating Pop Biscuits and Google Buns. The buns were most peculiar. They each had a very large currant in the middle, and this was filled with sherbet. So when you got to the currant and bit it the sherbet frothed out and filled your mouth with fine bubbles that tasted delicious. The children got a real surprise when they bit their currants, and Moon-Face almost fell off the branch with laughing.

"Come and see some new cushions I've got," he said to the children when they had eaten as many biscuits and buns as they could manage. Jo, Bessie and Fanny went into Moon-Face's funny round house.

Moon-Face looked round for Dick. But he wasn't there. "Where's Dick?" he said.

"He's gone up the ladder to peep and see what land is at the top," said Silky. "I told him not to. But he's rather a naughty boy, I think."

"Gracious!" said Jo, running out of the house. "Dick! Come back, you silly!"

Everyone began to shout, "Dick! DICK!"

But no answer came down the ladder. The big white cloud swirled above silently, and nobody could imagine why Dick didn't come back.

"I'll go and see what he's doing," said Moon-Face. So up he went. And he didn't come back either! Then the old Saucepan Man went cautiously up, step by step. He disappeared through the hole – and *he* didn't come back!

"Whatever has happened to them?" said Jo in the gravest astonishment. "Look here, girls – get a rope out of Moon-Face's house and tie yourselves and Silky to me. Then I'll go up the ladder —and if anyone tries to pull me into the land above, they won't be able to, because you three can pull me back. See?"

"Right," said Bessie, and she knotted the rope round her waist and Fanny's, and then round Silky's, too. Jo tied the other end to himself. Then up the ladder he went.

And before the girls quite knew what had happened, Jo was lifted into the land above—and they were all dragged up, too, their feet scrambling somehow up the ladder and through the hole in the cloud!

There they all stood in a field of red poppies, with a tall man nearby, holding a sack over his shoulder!

"Is that the lot?" he asked. "Good! Well, here's something to make you sleep!"

He put his hand in his sack and scattered a handful of the finest sand over the surprised group. In a trice they were rubbing their eyes and yawning.

"This is the Land of Dreams," said Moon-Face sleepily. "And that's the Sandman. Goodness, how sleepy I am!"

"Don't go to sleep! Don't go to sleep!" cried Silky, taking Moon-Face's arm and shaking him. "If we do, we'll wake up and find that this land has moved away from the Faraway Tree. Come back down the hole, Moon-Face, and don't be silly."

"I'm so – sleepy," said Moon-Face, and lay down among the red poppies. In a trice he was snoring loudly, fast asleep.

"Get him to the hole!" cried Silky. But Jo, Dick and the Saucepan Man were all yawning and rubbing their eyes, too sleepy to do a thing. Then Bessie and Fanny slid down quietly into the poppies and fell asleep, too. At last only Silky was left. Not much of the sleepy sand had gone into her eyes, so she was wider awake than the rest.

She stared at everyone in dismay. "Oh dear," she said, "I'll never get you down the hole by myself. I'll have to get help. I must go and fetch Watzisname and the Angry Pixie and Dame Washalot, too!"

She ran off to the hole, slipped down the ladder through the cloud and slid on to the broad branch below. "Watzisname!" she called. "Dame Washalot! Angry Pixie!"

After a minute or two Jo woke up. He rubbed his eyes and sat up. Not far off he saw something that pleased him very much indeed. It was an ice-cream man with his cart. The man was ringing his bell loudly.

"Hie, Moon-Face! Wake up!" cried Jo. "There's an ice-cream man. Have you any money?"

Everyone woke up. Moon-Face felt in his purse and then stared in the greatest surprise. It was full of marbles!

"Now who put marbles there?" he wondered.

The ice-cream man rode up. "Marbles will do

to pay for my ice-cream," he said. So Moon-Face paid him six marbles.

The man gave them each a packet and rode off, ringing his bell. Moon-Face undid his packet, expecting to find a delicious ice-cream there – but inside there was a big whistle! It was most astonishing.

Everyone else had a whistle, too. "How extraordinary!" said Dick. "This is the kind of thing that happens in dreams!"

"Well – after all – this *is* Dreamland!" said Bessie. "I wonder if these whistles blow!"

She blew hers. It was very loud indeed. The others blew theirs, too. And at once six policemen appeared near by, running for all they were worth. They rushed up to the children.

"What's the matter?" they cried. "You are blowing police whistles! What has happened? Do you want help?"

"No," said Dick with a giggle.

"Then you must come to the swimming-bath," said the policeman, and to everyone's enormous astonishment they were all led off.

"Why the *swimming* bath?" said Fanny. "Listen, policeman – we haven't got bathing costumes."

"Oh, you naughty story-teller!" said the policeman nearest to her.

And to Bessie's tremendous surprise she found that she had on a blue and white bathing costume – and all the others had bathing suits, too. It was most extraordinary.

They came to the swimming bath – but there

was no water in it at all. "Get in and swim," said the policeman.

"There's no water," said Dick. "Don't be silly." And then, very suddenly, all the policemen began to cry—and in a trice the swimming bath was full of their tears!

"This sort of thing makes me feel funny," said Jo. "I don't want to swim in tears. Quick, everyone—push the policemen into the bath!"

And in half a second all the policemen were kicking feebly in the bath of tears. As the children watched they changed into blue fishes and swam away, flicking their tails.

"I feel as if I'm in a dream," said Dick.

"So do I," said Jo. "I wish I could get out of it. Oh, look—there's an aeroplane coming down. Perhaps we could get into it and fly away!"

The aeroplane, which was small and green, landed near by. There was nobody in it at all. The children ran to it and got in. Jo pushed down the handle marked UP.

"Off we go!" he said. And off they went!

X

A FEW MORE ADVENTURES

Everyone was very pleased to be in the aeroplane, because they thought they could fly away from the Land of Dreams. After a second or two Bessie leaned over the side of the aeroplane to see how high they were from the ground. She gave a loud cry.

"What's the matter?" asked Jo.

"Jo! This isn't an aeroplane after all!" said Bessie in astonishment. "It's a bus. It hasn't got wings any more. Only wheels. And we're sitting on seats at the top of the bus. Well! I *did* think it was an aeroplane!"

"Gracious! Aren't we flying, then?" said Jo.

"No – just running down a road," said Fanny.

Everyone was silent. They were so disappointed. Then a curious noise was heard. Splishy-splash! Splash! Splash!

The children looked over the side of the bus – and they all gave a shout of amazement.

"Jo! Look! The bus is running on water! But it isn't a bus any more. Oh, look – it's got a sail!"

In the greatest astonishment everyone looked upwards – and there, billowing in the wind, was a great white sail. And Jo was now steering with a tiller instead of with a handle or a wheel. It was all most muddling.

"This is certainly the Land of Dreams, no doubt about that," groaned Jo, wondering whatever the ship would turn into. "The awful part is—we're awake—and yet we have to have these dream-like things happening!"

An enormous wave splashed over everyone. Fanny gave a scream. The ship rocked to and fro, to and fro, and everyone clung tightly to one another.

"Let's land somewhere, for goodness' sake!" cried Dick. "Goodness knows what this ship will turn into next—a rocking-horse, I should think, by the way it's rocking itself to and fro."

And do you know, no sooner had Dick said that than it did turn into a rocking-horse. Jo found himself holding on to its mane, and all the others clung together behind him. The water disappeared.

The rocking-horse seemed to be rocking down a long road.

"Let's get off," shouted Jo. "I don't like the way this thing keeps changing. Slip off, Moon-Face, and help the others down."

It wasn't long before they were all standing in the road, feeling rather queer. The rocking-horse went on rocking by itself down the road. As the children watched it, it changed into a large brown bear that scampered on its big paws.

"Ha!" said Jo. "We got off just in time! Well – what are we going to do now?"

A man came down the road carrying a green-covered tray on his head. He rang a bell. "Muffins! Fine muffins!" he shouted. "Muffins for sale!"

"Oooh! I feel exactly as if I could eat a muffin," said Bessie. "Hie, muffin-man! We'll have six muffins."

The muffin-man stopped. He took down his tray from his head and uncovered it. Underneath were not muffins, but small kittens!

The muffin-man seemed to think they were muffins. He handed one to each of the surprised children, and one to Moon-Face and Saucepan. Then he covered up his tray again and went down the road ringing his bell.

"Well, does he suppose we can eat kittens?" said Bessie. "I say – aren't they darlings? What are we going to do with them?"

"They seem to be growing," said Jo in surprise. And so they were. In a minute or two the kittens were too heavy to carry – they were big cats!

They still went on growing, and soon they were as big as tigers. They gambolled playfully round the children, who were really rather afraid of them.

"Now listen," said Jo to the enormous kittens. "You belong to the muffin-man. You go after him and get on to his tray where you belong. Listen – you can still hear his bell! Go along now!"

To everyone's surprise and delight the great animals gambolled down the road after the muffin-man.

"He *will* get a surprise," said Dick with a giggle. "I say – don't let's buy anything from anyone else. It's a bit too surprising."

"What we really ought to do is to try and find the hole that leads from this land to the Faraway Tree," said Jo seriously. "Surely you don't want to stay in this peculiar land for ever! Gracious, we never know what is happening from one minute to another!"

"I feel terribly sleepy again," said Moon-Face, yawning. "I do wish I could go to bed."

Now, as he said that, there came a clippitty-cloppitty noise behind them. They all turned – and to their great amazement saw a big white bed following them, tippitting along on four fat legs.

"Golly!" said Dick, stopping in surprise. "Look at that bed! Where did it come from?"

The bed stopped just by them. Moon-Face yawned.

"I'd like to cuddle down in you and go to sleep," he said to the bed. The bed creaked as if it was pleased.

Moon-Face climbed on to it. It was soft and cosy. Moon-Face put his head on the pillow and shut his eyes. He began to snore very gently.

This made everyone else feel dreadfully tired and sleepy, too. One by one they climbed into the big bed and lay down, snuggled together. The bed creaked in a very pleased way. Then it went on its way again, clippitty-clopping on its four fat legs, taking the six sleepers with it.

Now what had happened to Silky? Well, she had found Dame Washalot, Mister Watzisname and the Angry Pixie, and had told them how the others had fallen asleep in the Land of Dreams.

"Gracious! They'll never get away from there!" said Watzisname anxiously. "We must rescue them. Come along."

Dame Washalot put a wash-tub of water on her head. The Angry Pixie picked up a kettle of water. Watzisname didn't take anything. They all went up to the ladder at the top of the tree.

"The Land of Dreams is still here," said Silky when her head peeped over the top. "I can't see that horrid Sandman anywhere. It's a good chance to slip up and rescue the others now. Come on!"

Up they all went. They stared round the field of poppies, but they could see none of the others at all.

"We must hunt for them," said Silky. "Oh, my goodness, look at that great brown bear rushing along! I wonder if he knows anything about the others." She called out to him, but he didn't stop. He made a noise like a hen and rushed on.

The four of them wandered on and on – and suddenly they saw something most peculiar coming towards them – something wide and white.

"What in the world can it be?" said Silky in wonder. "Goodness me – it's a BED!"

And so it was – the very bed in which the four children and Moon-Face and Saucepan were asleep!

"Oh, look, look, look!" squealed Silky. "They're all here! Wake up, sillies! Wake up!"

But they wouldn't wake. They just sighed a little and turned over. Nothing that Silky and the others could do would wake them. And, in the middle of all this, there came footsteps behind them.

Silky turned and gave a squeal. "Oh, it's the Sandman! Don't let him throw his sand into your eyes or you will go to sleep, too! Quick, quick, do something!"

The Sandman was already dipping his hand into his big sack to throw sand into their eyes. But, quick as lightning, Dame Washalot picked up her wash-tub and threw the whole of the water over the sack! It wetted the sand so that the Sandman couldn't throw it properly. Then the Angry Pixie emptied his kettle over the Sandman himself, and he began to choke and splutter.

Watzisname stared. He suddenly took out his pocket-knife and slit a hole at the very bottom of the sack. The sand was dry there. Watzisname took a handful of it and threw it straight into the choking Sandman's eyes.

"Now *you* go to sleep for a bit!" shouted Watzisname. And, of course, that's just what the big Sandman did! He sank down under a bush and shut his eyes. His sleepy sand acted on him as much as on anyone else!

"Now we've got a chance!" said Silky, pleased. "Help me to wake everyone!"

But, you know, they just would *not* wake! It was dreadful.

"Well, we can't possibly get the bed down the hole," said Silky in despair. Then a bright idea came to her. She felt in Jo's pockets. She turned out the little pink jar of Whizz-Away ointment. "There may be *just* a little left!" she said.

And so there was – the very tiniest dab! "I hope it's enough!" said Silky. "Get on the bed, Dame Washalot and you others. I'm going to try a little magic. Ready?"

She rubbed the dab of ointment on to the head of the bed. "Whizz-Away Home, bed!" she said.

And, good gracious me, that big white bed whizzed away! It whizzed away so fast that Silky nearly fell off. It rushed through the air, giving all the birds a most terrible scare.

After a long time it came to the end of the Land of Dreams. A big white cloud stretched out at the edge. The bed flew through it, down and down. Then it flew in another direction.

"It's going back to the Faraway Tree, I'm sure," said Silky. And so it was! It arrived there and tried to get through the branches. It stuck on one and slid sideways. Everyone began to slide off.

"Wake up, wake up!" squealed Silky, banging the children and Moon-Face and Saucepan. They woke up in a hurry, for they were no longer in Dreamland. They felt themselves falling and and caught hold of branches and twigs.

"Where are we?" cried Dick. "What has happened?"

"Oh, goodness, too many things to tell you all at once," said Silky. "Is everyone safe? Then for goodness' sake come into my house and sit down for a bit. I really feel quite out of breath!"

XI

UP THE TREE AGAIN

Everyone crowded into Silky's room inside the tree. "How did we get back to the tree?" asked Dick in amazement.

Silky told him. "We found you all asleep on that big bed, and we rubbed on it some of the Whizz-Away ointment, the very last bit left. And it whizzed away here. Oh, and we wetted the Sandman's sand so that he couldn't throw sand into our eyes and make us go to sleep."

"Watzisname was clever, too. He slit the bottom of the sack with his knife, found a handful of dry sand there and threw it at the Sandman himself!" said the Angry Pixie. "And he went right off to sleep and couldn't interfere with us any more!"

"It was all Dick's fault," said Jo. "We said we wouldn't go to any more lands—and he went up there and got caught by the Sandman. So of course we had to go after him."

"Sorry," said Dick. "Anyway, everything's all right now. I won't do it again."

"We'd better go home," said Bessie. "It must be getting late. Goodness knows when we'll come again, Silky. Good-bye, everyone. Come and see us if we don't come to see you."

They all slid down the slippery-slip at top speed. Then they walked home, talking about their latest adventure.

"It was so queer being awake and having dreams," said Fanny. "Do you remember the muffins that turned into kittens?"

"I wish a really *nice* land would come to the top of the tree," said Jo. "Like the Land of Take-What-You-Want. That was fun. I wonder if it will ever come again."

For about a week the children did not even go into the Enchanted Wood. For one thing they were very busy helping their parents, and for another thing they felt that they didn't want any more adventures for a little while.

And then a note came from Silky and Moon-Face. This is what it said:

"DEAR BESSIE, FANNY, JO AND DICK,

"We know that you don't want any more adventures just yet, but you might like to know that there is a most exciting land at the top of the Faraway Tree just now. It is the Land of Do-As-You-Please, even nicer than the Land of Take-What-You-Want. We are going there to-night. If you want to come, come just before midnight and you can go with us. We will wait for you till then.

"Love from

"SILKY AND MOON-FACE."

The children read the note one after another. Their eyes began to shine.

"Shall we go?" said Fanny.

"Better not," said Jo. "Something silly is sure

to happen to us. It always does."

"Oh, Jo! Do let's go!" said Bessie. "You know how exciting the Enchanted Wood is at night, too, with all the fairy folk about—and the Faraway Tree lit with lanterns and things. Come on, Jo—say we'll go."

"I really think we'd better not," said Jo. "Dick might do something silly again."

"I would *not*!" said Dick in a temper. "It's not fair of you to say that."

"Don't quarrel," said Bessie. "Well, listen—if you don't want to go, Jo, Fanny and I will go with Dick. He can look after us."

"Pooh! Dick wants looking after himself," said Jo.

Dick gave Jo a punch on the shoulder and Jo slapped back.

"Oh, don't!" said Bessie. "You're not in the Land of Do-As-You-Please now!"

That made everyone laugh. "Sorry, Jo," said Dick. "Be a sport. Let's all go to-night. Or at any rate, let's go up the tree and hear what Silky and Moon-Face can tell us about this new land. If it sounds at all dangerous we won't go. See?"

"All right," said Jo, who really did want to go just as badly as the others, but felt that he ought not to keep leading the girls into danger. "All right. We'll go up and talk to Silky and Moon-Face. But mind—if I decide not to go with them, there's to be no grumbling."

"We promise, Jo," said Bessie. And so it was settled. They would go to the Enchanted Wood that night and climb the Faraway Tree to see their friends.

It was exciting to slip out of bed at half-past eleven and dress. It was very dark because there was no moon.

"We shall have to take a torch," said Jo. "Are you girls ready? Now don't make a noise, or you'll wake Mother."

They all crept down stairs and out into the dark, silent garden. An owl hooted nearby, and something ran down the garden path. Bessie nearly squealed.

"Sh! It's only a mouse or something," said Jo. "I'll switch on my torch now. Keep close together and we shall all see where we're going."

In a bunch they went down the back garden and out into the little lane there. The Enchanted Wood loomed up big and dark. The trees spoke to one another softly. "Wisha, wisha, wisha," they said. "Wisha, wisha, wisha!"

The children jumped over the ditch and walked through the wood, down the paths they knew so well. The wood was full of fairy folk going about their business. They took no notice of the children. Jo soon switched off his torch. Lanterns shone everywhere and gave enough light to see by.

They soon came to the great dark trunk of the Faraway Tree. A rope swung down through the branches.

"Oh, good!" said Dick. "Is Moon-Face going to pull us up?"

"No," said Jo. "We'll have to climb up—but

we can use the rope to help us. It's always in the tree at night to help the many folk going up and down."

And indeed there were a great many people using the Faraway Tree that night. Strange pixies, goblins and gnomes swarmed up and down it, and brownies climbed up, chattering hard.

"Where are they going?" asked Dick in surprise.

"Oh, up to the Land of Do-As-You-Please, I expect," said Jo. "And some of them are visiting their friends in the tree. Look – there's the Angry Pixie! He's got a party on to-night!"

The Angry Pixie had about eight little friends squashed into his tree-room, and looked as pleased as could be. "Come and join us!" he called to Jo.

"We can't," said Jo. "Thanks all the same. We're going up to Moon-Face's."

Everyone dodged Dame Washalot's washing water, laughed at old Watzisname sitting snoring as usual in his chair, and at last came to Moon-Face's house.

And there was nobody there! There was a note stuck on the door.

"We waited till midnight and you didn't come. If you do come and we're not here, you'll find us in the Land of Do-As-You-Please.

"Love from

"SILKY AND MOON-FACE."

"*P.S.* – DO come. Just *think* of the things you want to do – you can do them all in the Land of Do-As-You-Please!"

"Golly!" said Dick, longingly, "what I'd like to do better than anything else is to ride six times on a roundabout without stopping!"

"And *I'd* like to eat six ice-creams without stopping!" said Bessie.

"And *I'd* like to ride an elephant," said Fanny.

"And *I* should like to drive a motor-car all by myself," said Jo.

"Jo! *Let's* go up the ladder!" begged Fanny.

"Oh, do, do let's! Why can't we go and visit a really nice land when one comes? It's just too mean of you to say we can't."

"Well," said Jo. "Well – I suppose we'd better! Come on!"

With shrieks and squeals of delight the girls and Dick pressed up the little ladder, through the cloud. A lantern hung at the top of the hole to give them light – but, lo and behold! as soon as they had got into the land above the cloud it was daytime! How extraordinary!

The children stood and gazed round it. It seemed a very exciting land, rather like a huge amusement park. There were roundabouts going round and round in time to music. There were swings and see-saws. There was a railway train puffing along busily, and there were small aeroplanes flying everywhere, with brownies, pixies and goblins having a fine time in them.

"Goodness! Doesn't it look exciting?" said Bessie. "I wonder where Moon-Face and Silky are."

"There they are – over there – on that roundabout!" cried Jo. "Look – Silky is riding a tiger that is going up and down all the time – and Moon-Face is on a giraffe! Let's get on, too!"

Off they all ran. As soon as Moon-Face and Silky saw the children, they screamed with joy and waved their hands. The roundabout stopped and the children got on. Bessie chose a white rabbit. Fanny rode on a lion and felt very grand. Jo went on a bear and Dick chose a horse.

"So glad you came!" cried Silky. "We waited and waited for you. Oh – we're off! Hold tight!"

The roundabout went round and round and round. The children shouted for joy, because it went so fast. "Let's have six rides without getting off!" cried Jo. So they did – and dear me, weren't they giddy when they did at last get off. They rolled about like sailors!

"I feel like sitting down with six ice-creams," said Bessie. At once an ice-cream man rode up and handed them out thirty-six ice-creams. It did look a lot. When Jo had divided them all out equally there were six each. And how delicious they were! Everybody managed six quite easily.

"And now, what about me driving that railway engine!" cried Jo, jumping up. "I've always wanted to do that. Would you all like to be my passengers? Well, come on, then!"

And off they all raced to where the railway train was stopping at a little station. "Hi! hie!" yelled Jo to the driver. "I want to drive your train!"

"Come along up, then," said the driver, jumping down. "The engine is just ready to go!"

XII

THE LAND OF DO-AS-YOU-PLEASE

Jo jumped up into the cab of the engine. A bright fire was burning there. He looked at all the shining handles and wheels.

"Shall I know which is which?" he asked the driver.

"Oh, yes," said the driver. "That's the starting wheel – and that's to make the whistle go – and that's to go slow – and that's to go fast. You can't make a mistake. Don't forget to stop at the stations, will you? And oh – look out for the level-crossing gates, in case they are shut. It would be a pity to bump into them and break them."

Jo felt tremendously excited. Dick looked up longingly. "Jo! Could I come too?" he begged. "Do let me. Just to watch you."

"All right," said Jo. So Dick hopped up on to the engine. The girls, Moon-Face and Silky got into a carriage just behind. The guard ran up the platform waving a green flag and blowing his whistle.

"The signal's down!" yelled Dick. "Go on, Jo! Start her up!"

Jo twisted the starting wheel. The engine began to chuff-chuff-chuff and moved out of the station. The girls gave a squeal of delight.

"Jo's really driving the train!" cried Bessie. "Oh isn't he clever! He's wanted to drive an engine all his life!"

The engine began to go very fast—too fast. Jo pulled the "Go Slow" handle, and it went more slowly. He was so interested in what he was doing that he didn't notice he was coming to a station. He shot right through it!

"Jo!" cried Dick, "you've gone by a station. Gracious, the passengers waiting there did look cross—and oh, look, a lot of them in our train wanted to get out there!"

Sure enough quite a number of angry people were looking out of the carriage windows, yelling to Jo to stop.

Jo went red. He pulled the "Stop" handle. The engine stopped. Then Jo pulled the "Go Backwards" handle and the train moved slowly backwards to the station. It stopped there and Jo and Dick had the pleasure of seeing the passengers get out and in. The guard came rushing up.

"You passed the station, you passed the station!" he cried. "Don't you dare to pass my station again without stopping!"

"All right, all right," said Jo. "Now then—off we go again!" And off they went.

"Keep a look-out for stations, signals, tunnels and level crossings, Dick," said Jo. So Dick stuck his head out and watched.

"Level crossing!" he cried. "The gates are shut! Slow down, Jo, slow down!"

But unluckily Jo pulled the "Go Fast" handle instead of the "Go-Slow" and the train shot quickly to the closed gates of the level-crossing. Just as the engine had nearly reached them a

little man rushed out of the cabin near by and flung the gates open just in time!

"You bad driver!" he shouted as the train roared past. "You might have broken my gates!"

"That was a narrow squeak," said Jo. "What's this coming now, Dick?"

"A tunnel," said Dick. "Whistle as you go through in case anyone is walking in it."

So Jo made the engine whistle loudly. It really was fun. It raced through the dark tunnel and came out near a station.

"Stop! Station, Jo!" cried Dick. And Jo stopped. Then on went the train again, whistling loudly, rushing past signals that were down.

Then something happened. The "Go Slow" and the "Stop" handles wouldn't work! The train raced on and on past stations, big and small, through tunnels, past signals that were up, and behaved just as if it had gone mad.

"I say!" said Dick in alarm, "what's gone wrong, Jo?"

Jo didn't know. For miles and miles the train tore on, and all the passengers became alarmed. And then, as the train drew near a station, it gave a loud sigh, ran slowly and then stopped all by itself.

And it was the very same station it had started from! The driver of the train was there, waiting.

"So you're back again," he said. "My, you've been quick."

"Well, the engine didn't behave itself very well," said Jo, stepping down thankfully. "It just ran away the last part of the journey. It wouldn't stop anywhere!"

"Oh, I dare say it wanted to get back to me," said the driver, climbing into the engine-cab. "It's a monkey sometimes. Come along and drive it again with me."

"No, thank you," said Jo. "I think I've had enough. It was fun, though."

The girls, Moon-Face and Silky, got out of their carriages. They had been rather frightened the last part of the journey, but they thought Jo was very clever to drive the train by himself.

They all left the station. "Now what shall we do?" said Moon-Face.

"I want to ride on an elephant," said Fanny at once.

"There aren't any," said Bessie. But no sooner had she spoken than the children saw six big grey elephants walking solemnly up to them, swaying a little from side to side.

"Oh, look, look!" yelled Fanny, nearly mad with excitement. "There are my elephants. Six of them! We can all have a ride!"

Each elephant had a rope ladder up its left side. The children, Moon-Face and Silky climbed up and sat on a comfortable seat on the elephant's backs. Then the big creatures set off, swaying through the crowds.

It was simply lovely. Fanny did enjoy herself. She called to the others. "Wasn't this a good idea of mine, everybody? Aren't we high up? And isn't it fun?"

"It *is* fun," said Moon-Face, who had never even seen an elephant before, and would certainly never have thought of riding on one if he had. "Oh, goodness – my rope ladder has slipped off my elephant! Now I shall never be able to get down! I'll have to ride on this elephant all my life long!"

Everybody laughed – but Moon-Face was really alarmed. When the children had had enough of riding they all climbed down their rope ladders – but poor Moon-Face sat up high, tears pouring down his fat cheeks.

"I tell you I can't get down," he kept saying. "I'm up here for good!"

The elephant stood patiently for a little while. Then it got tired of hearing Moon-Face cry. It swung its enormous trunk round, wound it gently round Moon-Face's waist, and lifted him down to the ground. Moon-Face was so surprised that he couldn't speak a word.

At last he found his tongue. "What did the elephant lift me down with?" he asked. "His nose!"

"No, his trunk," said Jo, laughing. "Didn't you know that elephants had trunks, Moon-Face?"

"No," said Moon-Face, puzzled. "I'm glad he didn't pack me in his trunk and take me away for luggage!"

The children roared with laughter. They watched the big elephants walking off.

"What shall we do now?" said Jo. "Dick, what do you want to do?"

"Well, I know I can't do it—but wouldn't I just love to have a paddle in the sea!" said Dick.

"Oooh—that *would* be nice!" said Fanny, who loved paddling too. "But there isn't any sea here."

Just as she said that she noticed a sign-post near by. It pointed away from them and said, in big letters, "TO THE SEA."

"Goodness!" said Fanny. "Look at that! Come on, everyone!"

Off they all went, running the way that the sign-post pointed. And, after going round two corners, there, sure enough, was the blue, blue sea, lying bright and calm in the warm sunshine! Shining golden sands stretched to the little waves.

"Oh, goody, goody!" cried Dick, taking off his

shoes and socks at once. "Come on, quickly!"

Soon everyone was paddling in the warm sea. Moon-Face and Silky had never paddled before, but they loved it just as much as the children did. Dick paddled out so far that he got his shorts soaking wet.

"Oh, Dick! You *are* wet!" cried Bessie. "Come back!"

"This is the Land of Do-As-You-Please, isn't it?" shouted Dick, dancing about in the water and getting wetter than ever. "Well, I shall get as wet as I like, then!"

"Let's dig an ENORMOUS castle!" cried Moon-Face. "Then we can all sit on the top of it when the sea comes up."

"We can't," said Silky, suddenly looking sad.

"Why not? Why not?" cried Jo in surprise. "Isn't this the Land of Do-As-You-Please?"

"Yes," said Silky. "But it's time we went back to the Faraway Tree. This land will soon be on the move—and nice as it is, we don't want to live here for ever."

"Gracious, no," said Jo. "Our mother and father couldn't possibly do without us! Dick! Dick! Come in to shore! We're going home!"

Dick didn't want to be left behind. He waded back at once, his shorts dripping wet, and his jersey splashed, too. They all made their way to the hole that led down through the cloud to the Faraway Tree.

"We did have a lovely time," sighed Jo, looking back longingly at the gay land he was leaving behind. "It's one of the nicest lands that has ever been at the top of the Tree."

They all felt tired as they crowded into Moon-Face's room. "Don't fall asleep before you get home," said Moon-Face. "Take cushions, all of you."

They went down the slippery-slip, yawning. They made their way home and fell into bed, tired out but happy. And in the morning their mother spoke in surprise to Dick.

"Dick, how is it that your shorts and jersey are so wet this morning?"

"I paddled too deep in the sea," said Dick—and he couldn't *think* why his Aunt Polly said he was a naughty little story-teller!

XIII

THE LAND OF TOYS

One afternoon Silky came to see the children as they were all working hard in the garden. She leaned over the gate and called to them.

"Hallo! I've come to tell you something!"

"Oh, hallo, Silky dear!" cried everyone. "Come along in. We can't stop work because we've got to finish clearing this patch before tea."

Silky came in. She sat down on the barrow. "The old Saucepan Man wants to give a party," she said. "And he says, will you come?"

"Is it his birthday?" asked Jo.

"Oh, no. He doesn't know when his birthday is," said Silky. "He says he hasn't got one. This is just a party. You see, the Land of Goodies is coming soon, and Saucepan thought it would be a fine idea to go there with a large basket and collect as many good things to eat as he can find, and then give a party in Moon-Face's room, so that we can eat all the things."

"That sounds fine!" said Dick, who loved eating good things. "When shall we come?"

"To-morrow," said Silky. "About three o'clock. Will you be all right?"

"Oh, yes," said Bessie. "Mother says we've been very good this week, so she is sure to let us come to the Saucepan Man's party to-morrow. We'll be there! When is Saucepan going to get the goodies to eat?"

"To-morrow morning," said Silky. "He says that the Land of Goodies will be there then. Well, good-bye. I won't stay and talk to-day, as I said I'd make some Pop Biscuits and Google Buns for the tea to-morrow as well. I might make some Toffee Shocks, too."

Silky went. The children talked joyfully of the party next day.

"Hope there will be treacle pudding," said Dick.

"Treacle pudding! At a tea-party!" said Bessie.

"Well, why not?" said Dick. "It's most delicious. I hope there will be pink and yellow jelly, too."

Everyone felt excited when the next afternoon came. Mother said they might go, but she wouldn't let them put on their best clothes.

"Not if you are going to climb trees," she said. "And Dick, please don't get your clothes wet this time. If you do, you'll have to stay in bed all day whilst I dry them."

The children ran to the Enchanted Wood. They had to climb up the tree in the ordinary way, for there was no rope that day. Up they went, shouting a greeting to the owl in his room, to the Angry Pixie, and to Dame Washalot.

They reached Moon-Face's house. He and Silky were setting out cups and saucers and plates ready for all the goodies that Saucepan was going to bring back. Silky handed a bag round. "Have a Toffee Shock?" she said.

Now, all the children except Dick had had Toffee Shocks before, and, providing you knew, what the toffee did it was all right. But if you didn't, it was rather alarming.

A Toffee Shock gets bigger and bigger and bigger as you suck it, instead of smaller and smaller – and when it is so big that there is hardly room for it in your mouth it suddenly explodes – and goes to nothing. Jo, Bessie and Fanny watched Dick as he sucked his Toffee Shock, nudging one another and giggling.

Dick took a big Toffee Shock, for he was rather a greedy boy. He popped it into his mouth and sucked hard. It tasted most delicious. But it seemed to get bigger and bigger.

Dick tried to tell the others this, for it surprised him very much. But the Toffee Shock was now so big that he could hardly talk.

"Ooble, ooble, ooble!" he said.

"What language are you talking, Dick?" asked Moon-Face, with a giggle.

Dick looked really alarmed. His toffee was now so enormous that he could hardly find room in his mouth for it. And then suddenly it exploded—and his mouth was quite empty.

"Ooooh!" said Dick, opening and shutting his mouth like a goldfish. "Oooh!"

"Don't you like your sweet?" said Silky, trying not to giggle. "Well, spit it out if you like, and have another."

"It's gone!" said Dick. Then he saw the others laughing, and he guessed that Toffee Shocks were not quite the usual kind of sweets. He began to laugh, too. "Goodness, that did frighten me!" he said. "I say, wouldn't I like to give the master at my old school a Toffee Shock!"

Moon-Face looked at his clock. "Old Saucepan is a long time," he said. "It's half-past three now, and he promised to be really quick."

"Hallo—here's somebody coming now," said Moon-Face, hearing footsteps on the ladder that led up through the cloud. "Perhaps it's old Saucepan. But I can't hear his kettles clanking!"

Down the ladder came a wooden soldier. He saluted as he went past.

"Hie, hie!" shouted Moon-Face suddenly. "Wait a minute! How is it that you live in the Land of Goodies?"

"I don't," said the wooden soldier, in surprise. "I live in the Land of Toys."

"What! Is the Land of Toys up there now?" cried Moon-Face, standing up in astonishment.

"Of course!" said the soldier. "The Land of Goodies doesn't arrive till next week."

"Goodness!" groaned Moon-Face, as the soldier disappeared down the tree. "Old Saucepan has made a mistake. He's gone to the Land of Toys instead of to the Land of Goodies. I expect he is hunting everywhere for nice things to bring down to us – he's such a dear old stupid that he wouldn't know it wasn't the right land."

"We'd better go and tell him," said Silky. "You children can stay here till we come back, and then we'll have a nice tea of Pop Biscuits and Google Buns. Help yourself to Toffee Shocks whilst we are gone."

"We'll come too," said Bessie, jumping up. "The Land of Toys sounds exciting. I wish we'd brought Peronel, our doll. She would have loved to visit the Land of Toys."

"I suppose it isn't at all a dangerous land!" said Jo. "Just toys come alive?"

"Of course it's not dangerous," said Silky.

They all went up the ladder. They were very anxious to see what the Land of Toys was like. It was exactly as they imagined it!

Dolls' houses, toy sweet shops, toy forts, toy railway stations stood about everywhere, but much bigger than proper toys. Golliwogs, teddy bears, dolls of all kinds, stuffed animals and clockwork toys ran or walked about, talking and laughing.

"I say! This is fun!" said Bessie. "Oh, look at

those wooden soldiers all walking in a row!"

The children stared round, but Moon-Face pulled their arms.

"Come on," he said. "We've got to find out where the old Saucepan Man has got to! I can't see him anywhere."

The six of them wandered about the Land of Toys. Clockwork animals ran everywhere. A big Noah's Ark suddenly opened its lid and let out scores of wooden animals walking in twos. Noah came behind, humming.

The Saucepan Man was simply nowhere to be seen. "I'd better ask someone if they've seen him," said Moon-Face at last. So he stopped a big golliwog and spoke to him.

"Have you seen a little man hung about with kettles and saucepans?" he asked.

"Yes," said the golliwog at once. "He's bad. He tried to steal some sweets out of the sweet shop over there."

"I'm sure Saucepan wouldn't steal a thing!" said Jo angrily.

"Well, he did," said the golliwog. "I saw him."

"I know what happened," said Moon-Face, suddenly. "Old Saucepan thought this was the Land of Goodies. He didn't know it was the Land of Toys. So when he saw the sweet shop he thought he could take as many as he liked. You can in the Land of Goodies, you know. And people must have thought he was stealing."

"Oh, dear," said Silky, in dismay. "Golliwog, what happened to the Saucepan Man?"

"The policeman came up and took him off to prison," said the golliwog. "There's the policeman over there. You can ask him all about it."

The golliwog went off. The children, Moon-Face and Silky went over to the policeman. He told them it was quite true what the golliwog had said – Saucepan had tried to take sweets out of the sweet shop, and he had been locked up.

"Oh, we must rescue him!" cried Jo at once. "Where is he?"

"You must certainly not rescue him," said the policeman crossly. "I shan't tell you where he is!"

And no matter how much the children begged him, he would NOT tell them where he had put poor Saucepan.

"Well, we must just go and look for him ourselves, that's all," said Jo. And the six of them wandered off through the Land of Toys, shouting loudly as they went.

"Saucepan! Dear old Saucepan! Where are you?"

XIV

AN EXCITING RESCUE

The children, Moon-Face and Silky went down the crooked streets of the Land of Toys, calling the old Saucepan Man.

"Of course, Saucepan is very deaf," said Jo.

"He might not hear us calling him, even if he were locked up somewhere quite near."

They went on again, shouting and calling. The toys hurrying by stared at them in astonishment.

"Why do you keep calling 'Saucepan, Saucepan'?" asked a beautifully dressed doll. "Are you selling saucepans, or something?"

"No," said Jo. "We're looking for a friend."

Just then Silky heard something. She clutched Jo's arm. "Sh!" she said. "Listen! Do listen!"

Everyone stood still and listened. Then, floating on the air came a well-known voice, singing a silly song:

"Two trees in a teapot,
Two spoons in a pie,
Two clocks up the chimney.
Hi-tiddly-hie!"

"It's Saucepan!" cried Jo. "Nobody but Saucepan sings those silly songs. Where is he?"

They looked all round. There was a toy fort not far off, but, of course, much bigger than a proper toy fort. The song seemed to come from there.

"Two mice on a lamp-post,
Two hums in a bee,
Two shoes on a rabbit.
Hi-tiddly-hee!"

Jo laughed loudly. "I never knew such a stupid song in my life," he said. "I can't think how old Saucepan can make it up. It's coming from that fort. That's where he is locked up."

Everyone looked at the red-painted fort. Soldiers walked up and down on it. A drawbridge was pulled up so that no one could go in or out. When a soldier wanted to go out the drawbridge was let down and the soldier stepped over it. Then it was pulled up again.

"Well, Saucepan is certainly in there," said Moon-Face. "And, by the way, don't call to him, any of you. We don't want the guards to know that there are any friends of his here – else they may guess we'll try and rescue him."

"Oh, do let's try and let him know we're here," said Bessie. "He would be so very, very glad. He must feel so worried and unhappy."

"I know a way of telling him we are here, without anyone guessing we are friends of his," said Jo suddenly. "Listen."

He stood and thought for a moment. Then he raised his voice and sang a little song:

"Two boys in the high-road,
Two girls in the street,
Two friends feeling sorry.
Tweet-tweet-tweet-tweet-tweet!"

Everyone roared with laughter. "It's very clever, Jo," said Dick. "Two boys – Saucepan will know that's you and me – two girls – that's Bessie and Fanny – two friends, Silky and Moon-Face! Saucepan will know we're all here!"

A frightful noise came from the fort – a clanging and a banging, a clanking and crashing. Everyone listened.

"That's old Saucepan dancing round madly to let us know he heard and understood," said Jo. "Now the thing is – how are we going to rescue him?"

They walked down the street, talking, trying to think of some good way to save poor Saucepan. They came to a clothes shop. In it were dolls' clothes of all sorts. In the window was a set of sailor's clothes, too. Jo stared at them.

"Now, I wonder," he said. "I just wonder if they've got any soldier's clothes. Moon-Face, lend me your big purse if it's got any money in."

Moon-Face put his large purse into Jo's hand. Jo disappeared into the shop. He came out with three sets of bright red soldier's uniforms, with big, black, furry bearskins for hats.

"Come on," he said in excitement. "Come somewhere that we shan't be seen."

They all hurried down the street and came to a field where some toy cows stood grazing.

They climbed over the gate and went behind the hedge. "Dick, see if this uniform will fit you," said Jo. "I'll put this one on."

"But Jo–Jo–what are you going to do?" asked Bessie in surprise.

"I should have thought you could have guessed," said Jo, putting on the uniform quickly. "We're going to see if we can march into the fort and get old Saucepan out! I should think they will let down the drawbridge for us if we are dressed like soldiers."

"Is this third suit for me?" asked Moon-Face, excitedly.

"No, Moon-Face," said Jo. "I didn't think you'd look a bit like a soldier, even if you were dressed like one. You must stay outside and look after the girls. This third suit is for old Saucepan. The soldiers wouldn't let us take him out of the fort all hung round with kettles and saucepans! They would know it was the prisoner and would stop him. He'll have to take off his kettles and things and dress in this. Then, maybe we can rescue him quite easily."

"Jo, you are really very, very clever," said Silky.

Jo felt very pleased. He buckled his belt, and put on his black bearskin. My word, he did look grand! So did Dick.

"Now we're ready," said Jo. "Moon-Face, if by any chance Dick and I are caught, you must take the girls safely back to the Tree. See?"

"I see," said Moon-Face. "Good luck, boys!"

Everyone went out of the field and walked back to the fort. When they got near it, Dick and Jo began to march very well, indeed. Left, right, left, right, left, right!

They came to the fort. "Soldier, let down the drawbridge!" yelled Jo, in his loudest and most commanding voice. The sentinel peered over the wall of the fort. When he saw two such smart soldiers, he saluted at once, and set to work to let down the drawbridge. Crash! It fell flat to the ground, and Dick and Jo walked over it into the fort.

Creak, creeeee-eak! The drawbridge was drawn up again. Jo and Dick marched right into the fort. Soldiers saluted at once.

"I wish to talk to the prisoner here," said Jo.

"Yes, captain," said a wooden soldier, saluting. He took a key from his belt and gave it to Jo. "First door on the right, sir," he said. "Be careful. He may be fierce."

"Thanks, my man," said Jo, and marched to the first door on the right. He unlocked it and he and Dick went in and shut the door. Saucepan was there! When he saw the two soldiers, he fell on his knees.

"Set me free, set me free!" he begged. "I did not mean to steal the sweets. I thought this was the Land of Goodies."

"Saucepan! It's us!" whispered Jo, taking off his helmet so that Saucepan could see him plainly. "We've come to save you. Put on this uniform, quick!"

"But what about my kettles and saucepans?" said Saucepan. "I can't leave them behind."

"Don't be silly. You'll have to," said Jo. "Quick, Dick, help him off with them."

The two boys stripped off every pan and made Saucepan dress up in the red uniform. He trembled so much with excitement that they had to do up every button for him.

"Now march close to us and don't say a word," said Jo, when Saucepan was ready. His kettles and saucepans lay in a heap on the floor. He fell over them as he scrambled across to Jo and Dick. Jo opened the door. All three marched out, keeping in step. Left, right, left, right, left, right!

The other soldiers in the fort looked up but saw nothing but three of their comrades – or so they thought. Jo shouted to the sentinel:

"Let down the drawbridge!"

"Very good, captain!" cried the sentinel, and let it down with a crash. Jo, Dick and Saucepan marched out at once. Left, right, left, right, left, right.

Moon-Face and the girls could hardly believe that the third soldier was old Saucepan. He did look so different in uniform, without his pans hung all round him. Silky flew to hug him.

And then the sentinel of the fort yelled out in a loud voice: "I believe that's the prisoner! I believe he's escaped! Hie, hie, after them!"

"Goodness! Run! run!" cried Jo, at once. And they all ran. How they ran! Soldiers poured out of the fort after them, golliwogs and teddy bears joined in the chase, and dolls of all kinds pattered behind on their small feet.

"To the hole in the cloud!" shouted Jo. "Run, Bessie; run, Fanny! Oh, I do hope we get there in time!"

XV

A SHOCK FOR THE TOYS

How the children and the others ran! They knew quite well that if they were caught they would be put into the toy fort—and then the Land of Toys would move away from the Faraway Tree, and goodness knew how long they might have to stay there!

So they ran at top speed. Fanny fell behind a little, and Jo caught her hand to help her. Panting and puffing, they raced down the streets of the Land of Toys, trying to remember where the hole led down through the cloud to the Faraway Tree.

Jo remembered the way. He led them all to the hole—and there was the ladder, thank goodness! "Down you go!" cried the boy to Silky, Bessie and Fanny. "Hurry! Get into Moon-Face's room quickly."

Down the girls went, and then Dick, Moon-Face, Saucepan and Jo. Jo only just got down in time, for a large golliwog, with very long legs, had almost caught them up – and as Jo went down he reached out and tried to catch Jo's collar.

Jo jerked himself away. His collar tore – and the boy half slid, half climbed down the ladder to safety. Soon he was in Moon-Face's house with the others – but what was this? The toys did not stay up in their land – they poured down the ladder after the children and their friends!

"They're coming in here!" yelled Moon-Face. "Oh, why didn't we shut the door?"

But it was too late then to shut the door. Soldiers, golliwogs, bears and dolls poured into Moon-Face's funny round room – and Moon-Face, quick as lightning, gave them each a push towards the middle of his room.

The opening of his slippery-slip was there – and one by one all the astonished toys fell into the hole and found themselves sliding wildly down the inside of the tree!

As soon as Jo and the others saw what Moon-Face was doing, they did the same.

"Down you go!" said Jo to a fat golliwog, giving him a hard push – and down he went.

"A push for you!" yelled Dick to a big blue teddy bear – and down the slide went the bear.

Soon the children could do no more pushing, for they began to giggle. It really was too funny to see the toys rushing in, being pushed, and going down the slide, squealing and kicking for all they were worth. But after a while no more toys came, and Moon-Face shut his door. He flung himself on his curved bed, and laughed till the tears ran down his cheeks and wetted his pillow.

"What will the toys do?" asked Jo at last.

"Climb back up the tree to the Land of Toys," said Moon-Face, drying his eyes. "We'll see them out of my window. They won't interfere with us again!"

After about an hour the toys began to come past Moon-Face's window, slowly, as if they were tired. Not one of them tried to open the door and get into Moon-Face's house.

"They're afraid that if they don't get back into their land at once it will move away!" said Silky. "Let's sit here and watch them all – and have a few Google Buns and Pop Biscuits."

"I'm so very sorry to have caused all this trouble," said the Saucepan Man in a humble voice. "And I didn't bring anything back for tea either. You see, I really thought, when I got into the Land of Toys, that it was the Land of Goodies, because one of the first things I saw was that toy sweet shop. And in the Land of Goodies you can just take anything you like without paying – so of course I went right into the shop and began to empty some chocolates out of a box. That's why they put me into prison. It was dreadful. Oh, I *was* glad to hear Jo singing. I knew at once that you would try to rescue me."

This was a very long speech for Saucepan to make. He looked so unhappy and sorry that everyone forgave him at once for making such a silly mistake.

"Cheer up, Saucepan," said Moon-Face. "The Land of Goodies will soon come along – and we'll ALL go and visit it, not just you – and we'll have the grandest feast we have ever had in our lives."

"Oh, but do you think we ought to?" began Jo. "Honestly, we seem to get into a fix every single time we go up the ladder."

"I'll make quite sure that the Land of Goodies is there," said Moon-Face. "Nothing whatever can go wrong if we visit it. Don't be afraid. I say, Jo, you and Dick and Saucepan do look awfully grand in your soldier's uniforms. Are you always going to wear them?"

"Oh, gracious – I forgot we haven't got our proper clothes," said Jo. "Mother will be cross if we leave them in the Land of Toys. We left them under a hedge near the fort."

"And I left my lovely kettles and saucepans in the fort," said Saucepan in a mournful voice. "I feel funny without them. I don't like being a soldier. I want to be a Saucepan Man."

"I'd like you to be our dear old Saucepan Man, too," said Silky. "It doesn't seem you, somehow, dressed up like that. But I don't see how we are to get anything back. Certainly none of us is going back into the Land of Toys again!"

Just then three sailor dolls, last of all the toys, came climbing slowly up the tree. They were crying. Their sailor clothes were torn and soaking wet.

Moon-Face opened his door. "What's the matter?" he asked. "What's happened to you?"

"Awful things," said the first sailor. "We were climbing up this tree when we came to a window, and we all peeped in. And a very angry pixie flew out at us and pushed us off the branch. The Faraway Tree was growing thorns just there and they tore our clothes to bits. And then a whole lot of washing water came pouring down the tree on top of us and soaked us. So we feel dreadful. If only we could get some new clothes!"

"Listen!" cried Jo suddenly. "How would you like to have our soldier uniforms? They are quite new and very smart."

"Oooh!" said all the sailor dolls together. "We'd love that. Would you really give us those? We shall get into such trouble if we go back to the Land of Toys like this."

"We'll give you them on one condition, sailor dolls," said Jo. "You must find our own things in the Land of Toys and throw them down the ladder to us. We'll tell you where they are."

"We can easily do that," promised the sailors. So Jo, Dick and the Saucepan stripped off their smart uniforms and gave them to the sailor dolls who took off their torn blue clothes and dressed themselves in the red trousers, tunics and bearskin helmets. They looked as smart as could be.

"Now you *will* find our clothes for us, won't you?" said Jo. "We are trusting you, you see."

"We are very trustable," said the dolls, and ran up the ladder after Jo had told them exactly where to find everything.

Jo, Dick and Saucepan sat in their vests and pants and shivered a little, for the uniforms had been warm. "We shall look funny going home like this if those sailors don't keep their word!" said Dick. "As a matter of fact, I'd have liked to keep that uniform. I like it much better than my clothes."

"Look – something's coming down the ladder!" cried Moon-Face, and they all ran out to see. "How quick the sailor dolls have been – or soldier dolls, I suppose, we ought to call them now."

Two sets of clothes tumbled down the ladder and the children caught them. Then came a clatter and a clanging as kettles and saucepans came down too. Saucepan was delighted. He put on a pair of ragged trousers and a funny old coat that came down with the pans – and then Silky helped him to string his kettles and saucepans round him as usual.

"Now you look our dear old Saucepan again," said Silky. The boys dressed, too. Then Jo looked at Moon-Face's clock.

"We must go," he said. "Thanks for the Pop Biscuits and everything. Now, Saucepan, don't get into any more trouble for a little while!"

"Smile?" said Saucepan, going suddenly deaf again. "I *am* smiling. Look!"

"That's a grin, not a smile!" said Jo, as he saw

Saucepan smiling from ear to ear. "Now don't get into any more TROUBLE!"

"Bubble? Where's a bubble?" said Saucepan, looking all round. "I didn't see anyone blowing bubbles."

The children grinned. Saucepan was always very funny when he heard things wrong.

"Come on," said Bessie. "Mother will be cross if we're home too late. Good-bye, Moon-Face. Good-bye, Silky. We'll see you again soon."

"Well, don't forget to come to the Land of Goodies with us," said Silky. "That really will be fun. Nearly as much fun as the Land of Do-As-You-Please."

"We'll come," promised Bessie. "Don't go without us. Can I have a red cushion, Moon-Face? Thank you!"

One by one the four children slid swiftly down the slippery-slip to the bottom of the tree. They shot out of the trap-door, gave the red squirrel the cushions and set off home.

"I'm looking forward to our next adventure," said Dick. "It makes my mouth water when I think of the Land of Goodies! Hurrah!"

XVI

THE LAND OF GOODIES

The four children were rather naughty the next few days. Dick and Jo quarrelled, and they fell over when they began to wrestle with one another, and broke a little table.

Then Bessie scorched a table-cloth when she was ironing it – and Fanny tore an enormous hole in her blue frock when she went blackberrying.

"Really, you are all very naughty and careless lately," said their mother. "Jo, you will mend that table as best you can. Dick, you must help him – and if I see you quarrelling like that again I shall send you both to bed at once. Fanny, why didn't you put on your old overall when you went blackberrying, as I told you to? You are a naughty little girl. Sit down and mend that tear properly."

Bessie had to wash the table-cloth carefully to try and get the scorch marks out of it.

"I say, it's a pity all these things have happened just this week," groaned Jo to Dick, as the two boys did their best to mend the table. "I'm afraid the Land of Goodies will come and go before we get there! I daren't ask Mother or Father if we can go off to the Faraway Tree. We've been so naughty that they are sure to say no."

"Moon-Face and the others will be wondering why we don't go," said Bessie, almost in tears.

They were. The Land of Goodies had come, and a most delicious smell kept coming down the ladder. Moon-Face waited and waited for the children to come, and they didn't.

Then he heard that the Land of Goodies was going to move away the next afternoon, and he wondered what to do.

"We said we'd wait for the children – but we don't want to miss going ourselves," he said to Silky. "We had better send a note to them. Perhaps something has happened to stop them coming."

So they wrote a note, and went down to ask the owl to take it. But he was asleep. So they went to the woodpecker, who had a hole in the tree for himself, and he said he would take it.

He flew off with it in his beak. He soon found the cottage and rapped at the window with his beak.

"A lovely woodpecker!" cried Jo, looking up. "See the red on his head? He's got a note for us!"

He opened the window. Mother was there, ironing in the same room as the children, and she looked most astonished to see such an unexpected visitor.

Jo took the note. The bird stayed on the window-sill, waiting for an answer. Jo read it and then showed it to the others. They all looked rather sad. It was dreadful to know that the lovely Land of Goodies had come and was so soon going – and they couldn't visit it.

"Tell Moon-Face we've been naughty and can't come," said Jo.

The bird spread its wings, but Mother looked up

and spoke. "Wait a minute!" she said to the bird. Then she turned to Jo. "Read me the note," she said.

Jo read it out loud:

"DEAR JO, BESSIE, FANNY AND DICK,

"The Land of Goodies is here and goes to-morrow. We have waited and waited for you to come. If you don't come to-morrow we shall have to go by ourselves. Can't you come?

"Love from

"SILKY, SAUCEPAN AND MOON-FACE."

"The Land of Goodies!" said Mother in amazement. "Well, I never did hear of such funny happenings! I suppose there are lots of nice things to eat there, and that's why you all want to go. Well – you certainly have been bad children – but you've done your best to put things right. You may go to-morrow morning!"

"Mother! Oh, Mother, thank you!" cried the children. "Thank you, Aunt Polly!" said Dick, hugging her. "Oh, how lovely!"

"Tell Moon-Face we'll come as soon as we can to-morrow morning," said Jo to the listening woodpecker. He nodded his red-splashed head and flew off. The children talked together, excited.

"I shan't have any breakfast," said Bessie. "It's not much good going to the Land of Goodies unless we're hungry!"

"That's a good idea," said Dick. "I think I won't have any supper to-night either!"

So when the time came for the four children to

set off to the Enchanted Wood, they were all terribly hungry! They ran to the Faraway Tree and climbed up it in excitement.

"I hope there are treacle tarts," said Jo.

"I want chocolate blancmange," said Bessie.

"I simply can't begin to say the things I'd like," said greedy Dick.

"Well, don't," said Jo. "Save your breath and hurry. You're being left behind!"

They got to Moon-Face's, and shouted loudly to him. He came running out of his tree-house in delight.

"Oh, good, good, good!" he cried. "You *are* nice and early. Silky, they're here! Go down and call old Saucepan. He's with Mister Watzisname.

I'm sure Saucepan would like to come too."

It wasn't long before seven excited people were climbing up the ladder to the Land of Goodies. How they longed to see what it was like!

Well, it was much better than anyone imagined! It was a small place, set with little crooked houses and shops – and every single house and shop was made of things to eat! The first house that the children saw was really most extraordinary.

"Look at that house!" cried Jo. "Its walls are made of sugar – and the chimneys are chocolate – and the window-sills are peppermint cream!"

"And look at that shop!" cried Dick. "It's got walls made of brown chocolate, and the door is made of marzipan. And I'm sure the window-sills are gingerbread!"

The Land of Goodies was really a very extraordinary place. Everything in it seemed to be eatable. And then the children caught sight of the trees and bushes and called out in the greatest astonishment:

"Look! That tree is growing currant buns!"

"And that one has got buds that are opening out into biscuits! It's a Biscuit Tree!"

"And look at this little tree here – it's growing big, flat, white flowers like plates – and the middle of the flowers is full of jelly. Let's taste it."

They tasted it – and it *was* jelly! It was really most peculiar. There was another small bush that grew clusters of a curious-looking fruit, like flat berries of all colours – and, will you believe it, when the children picked the fruit it was boiled sweets, all neatly growing together like a bunch of grapes.

"Oooh, lovely!" said Jo, who liked boiled sweets very much. "I say, look at that yellow fence over there – surely it isn't made of barley-sugar!"

It was. The children broke off big sticks from the fence, and sucked the barley-sugar. It was the nicest they had ever tasted.

The shops were full of things to eat. You should just have seen them! Jo felt as if he would like a sausage roll and he went into a sausage-roll shop. The rolls were tumbling one by one out of a machine. The handle was being turned by a most peculiar man. He was quite flat and brown, and had what looked like black currants for eyes.

"Do you know. I think he is a gingerbread man!" whispered Jo to the others. "He's just like the gingerbread people that Mother makes for us."

The children chose a sausage roll each and went out, munching. They wandered into the next shop. It had lovely big iced cakes, set out in rows. Some were yellow, some were pink, and some white.

"Your name, please?" asked the funny little woman there, looking at Bessie, who had asked for a cake.

"Bessie," said the little girl in surprise. And there in the middle of the cake her name appeared in pink sugar letters! Of course, all the others wanted cakes, too, then, just to see their names come!

"We shall never be able to eat all these," said Moon-Face, looking at the seven cakes that had suddenly appeared. But, you know, they tasted so delicious that it wasn't very long before they all went!

Into shop after shop went the children and the others, tasting everything they could see. They had tomato soup, poached eggs, ginger buns, chocolate fingers, ice-creams, and goodness knows what else.

"Well, I just simply CAN'T eat anything more," said Silky at last. "I've been really greedy. I am sure I shall be ill if I eat anything else."

"Oh, Silky!" said Dick. "Don't stop. I can go on for quite a long time yet."

"Dick, you're greedy, *really* greedy," said Jo. "You ought to stop."

"Well, I'm not going to," said Dick. The others looked at him.

"You're getting very fat," said Jo suddenly. "You won't be able to get down the hole! You be careful, Dick. You are not to go into any more shops."

"All right," said Dick, looking sulky. But although he did not go into the shops, do you know what he did? He broke off some of a gingerbread window-sill – and then he took a knocker from a door. It was made of barley-sugar, and Dick sucked it in delight. The others had not seen him do these things – but the man whose knocker Dick had pulled off did see him!

He opened his door and came running out. "Hie, hie!" he cried angrily. "Bring back my knocker at once! You bad, naughty boy!"

XVII

DICK GETS EVERYONE INTO TROUBLE

When Jo and the others heard the angry voice behind them, they turned in surprise. Nobody but Dick knew what the angry little man was talking about.

"Knocker?" said Jo, in astonishment. "What knocker? We haven't got your knocker."

"That bad boy is eating my knocker!" cried the man, and he pointed to Dick. "I had a beautiful one, made of golden barley-sugar – and now that boy has eaten it nearly all up!"

They all stared at Dick. He went very red. What was left of the knocker was in his mouth.

"Did you really take his barley-sugar knocker?" said Jo in amazement. "Whatever were you thinking of, Dick?"

"Well, I just never thought," said Dick, swallowing the rest of the knocker in a hurry. "I saw it there on the door – and it looked so nice. I'm very sorry."

"That's all very well," said the angry man. "But being sorry won't bring back my knocker. You're a bad boy. You come and sit in my house till the others are ready to go. I won't have you going about in our land eating knockers and chimneys and window-sills!"

"You'd better go, Dick," said Jo. "We'll call for you when we're ready to go home. We shan't be long now. Anyway, you've eaten quite enough."

So poor Dick had to go into the house with the cross little man, who made him sit on a stool and keep still. The others wandered off again.

"We mustn't be here much longer," said Moon-Face. "It's almost time for this land to move on. Look! Strawberries and cream."

The children stared at the strawberries and cream. They had never seen such a strange sight before. The strawberries grew by the hundred on strawberry plants – but each strawberry had its own big dob of cream growing on it, ready to be eaten.

"They are even sugared!" said Jo, picking one. "Look – my strawberry is powdered with white sugar – and, oh, the cream is delicious!"

They enjoyed the strawberries and cream, and then Jo had a good idea.

"I say! What about taking some of these lovely goodies back with us?" he said. "Watzisname would love a plum pie – and the Angry Pixie would like some of those jelly-flowers – and Dame Washalot would like a treacle pudding."

"And Mother would like lots of things, too," said Bessie joyfully.

So they all began collecting puddings and pies and cakes. It was fun. The treacle pudding had so much treacle that it dripped all down Moon-Face's leg.

"You'll have to have a bath, Moon-Face," said Silky. "You're terriby sticky."

They nearly forgot to call for poor Dick! As they passed the house whose knocker he had eaten, he banged loudly on the window, and they all stopped.

"Gracious! We nearly forgot about Dick!" said Bessie. "Dick, Dick, come on! We're going!"

Dick came running out of the house. The little man called after him: "Now, don't you eat anybody's knocker again!"

"Goodness! Why have you got all those things?" asked Dick in surprise, looking at the puddings and pies and cakes. "Are they for our supper?"

"Dick! How can you think of supper after eating such a lot!" cried Jo. "Why, I'm sure I couldn't eat even a chocolate before to-morrow morning. No—these things are for Watzisname and Dame Washalot and Mother. Come on. Moon-Face says this land will soon be on the move."

They all went to the hole that led down through the cloud. It didn't take long to climb down the ladder and on to the big branch outside Moon-Face's house.

Dick came last—and he suddenly missed his footing and fell right down the ladder on the top of the others below. And he knocked the puddings, pies and cakes right out of their hands! Down went all the goodies, bumping from branch to branch. The children and the others stared after them in dismay.

Then there came a very angry yell from below. "Who's thrown a treacle pudding at me? Wait till I get them. I've treacle all over me. It burst on my head. Oh, oh, OH!"

Then there came an angry squealing from lower

down still. "Plum pie! Plum pie in my washtub! Sausage rolls in my washtub! Peppermints down my neck! Oh, you rascals up there – I'm coming up after you, so I am!"

And from still lower down came the voice of the Angry Pixie – and truly a very angry pixie, indeed, he was! "Jelly on my nose! Jelly down my neck! Jelly in my pockets! What next? Who's doing all this? Wait till I come up and tell them what I think!"

The children listened, half frightened and very much amused. They began to giggle.

"Plum pie in Dame Washalot's tub!" giggled Jo.

"Jelly on the Angry Pixie's nose!" said Bessie.

"I say – I do believe they really are coming up!" said Jo, in alarm. "Look – isn't that Watzisname?"

They all peered down the tree. Yes – it was Watzisname climbing up, looking very angry. The Saucepan Man leaned over rather too far, and nearly fell. Dick just caught him in time – but one of his kettles came loose and fell down. It bounced from branch to branch and landed on poor old Watzisname's big head!

He gave a tremendous yell. "What! Is it you, Saucepan, throwing all these things down the tree. What you want is a spanking. And you'll get it? And anybody else up there playing tricks will get a fine fat spanking, too!"

"A spanking!" said Dame Washalot's voice.

"A SPANKING!" roared the Angry Pixie not far behind.

"Golly!" said Jo in alarm. "It looks as if the Land of Spankings is about to arrive up here. I vote we go. You'd better shut your door, Moon-Face, and you and Silky and Saucepan had better lie down on the sofa and the bed and pretend to be asleep. Then maybe those angry people will think it's somebody up in the Land of Goodies that has been throwing all those things down."

"Dick ought to stay up there and get the spankings," said Moon-Face gloomily. "First he goes and eats somebody's door-knocker and gets into trouble. Then he falls on top of us all and sends all the goodies down the tree."

"I'm going down the slippery-slip with the children," said Silky, who was very much afraid of Mister Watzisname when he was in a temper. "I can climb up to my house and lock myself in before all those angry people come down again. Saucepan, why don't you come, too?"

Saucepan thought he would. So the children and Silky and Saucepan all slid down the slippery-slip. Just in time, too – for Mister Watzisname came shouting up to Moon-Face's door as Jo, who was last, slid down.

Moon-Face had shut his door. He was lying on his bed, pretending to be asleep. Watzisname banged hard on the door. Moon-Face didn't answer. Watzisname peeped in at the window.

"Moon-Face! Wake up! Wake up, I say!"

"What's the matter?" said Moon-Face, in a sleepy voice, sitting up and rubbing his eyes.

Dame Washalot and the Angry Pixie came up,

too. The Pixie had jelly all over him, and Watzisname had treacle pudding down him. They were all very angry.

They opened Moon-Face's door and went in. "Who was it that threw all those things down on us?" asked Watzisname. "Where's Saucepan? Did he throw that kettle? I'm going to spank him."

"Whatever are you talking about?" said Moon-Face, pretending not to know. "How sticky you are, Watzisname!"

"And so are you!" yelled Watzisname, suddenly, seeing treacle shining all down Moon-Face's legs. "It was you who threw that pudding down on me! My word, I'll spank you hard!"

Then all three of them went for poor Moon-Face, who got about six hard slaps. He rolled over to the slippery-slip, and slid down it in a fright.

He shot out of the trap-door just in time to see Silky and Saucepan saying good-bye to the children. They were most amazed when Moon-Face shot out beside them.

"I've been spanked!" wept Moon-Face. "They all spanked me because I was sticky, so they thought I'd thrown all the goodies at them. And now I'm afraid to go back because they will be waiting for me."

"Poor Moon-Face," said Jo. "And it was all Dick's fault. Listen. Silky can climb back to her house; but you and Saucepan had better come back with us and stay the night. Dick and I will sleep downstairs on the sofa, and you can have our beds. Mother won't mind."

"All right," said Moon-Face, wiping his eyes. "That will be fun. Oh, what a pity we wasted all those lovely goodies! I really do think Dick is a clumsy boy!"

They all went home together, and poor Dick didn't say a word. But how he did wish he could make up for all he had done!

XVIII

A SURPRISING VISITOR

The children's mother was rather astonished to see Moon-Face and Saucepan arriving at the cottage with the children.

"Mother, may they stay the night?" asked Jo. "They've been so good to us in lots of ways – and they don't want to go back to the tree to-night because somebody is waiting there to spank them."

"Dear me!" said Mother, even more surprised. "Well, yes, they can stay. You and Dick must sleep downstairs on the sofa. If they like to help in the garden for a day or two, they can stay longer."

"Oooh!" said Moon-Face, pleased. "That would be fine! I'm sure Watzisname will have forgotten about spanking us if we can stay away a few days. Thank you very much. We will help all we can."

"Would you like one of my very special kettles?" asked Saucepan gratefully. "Or a fine big saucepan for cooking soup bones?"

"Thank you," said Mother, smiling, for the old Saucepan Man was really a funny sight, hung about as usual with all his pans. "I could do with a strong little kettle. But let me pay you."

"Certainly not, madam," said Saucepan, hearing quite well for a change. "I shall be only too pleased to present you with anything you like in the way of kettles or saucepans."

He gave Mother a fine little kettle and a good strong saucepan. She was very pleased. Moon-Face looked on, wondering what he could give her, too. He put his hand in his pocket and felt around a bit. Then he brought out a bag and offered it to the children's mother.

"Have a bit of toffee?" he asked. Mother took a piece. The children stared at her, knowing that it was a piece of Shock Toffee! Poor Mother!

The toffee grew bigger and bigger and bigger in her mouth as she sucked it, and she looked more and more surprised. At last, when she felt that it was just as big as her whole mouth, it exploded into nothing at all–and the children squealed with laughter.

"Mother, that was a Toffee Shock!" said Jo, giggling. "Would you like to try a Pop Biscuit–or a Google Bun?"

"No, thank you," said Mother at once. "The Toffee Shock tasted delicious–but it *did* give me a shock!"

It *was* fun having Moon-Face and Saucepan staying with them in their cottage for a few days. The children simply loved it. Moon-Face was very,

very good in the garden, for he dug and cleared away rubbish twice as fast as anyone else. The old Saucepan Man wasn't so good because he suddenly went deaf again and didn't understand what was said to him. So he did rather queer things.

When Mother said: "Saucepan, fetch me some carrots, will you?" he thought she had asked for sparrows, and he spent the whole morning trying to catch them by throwing salt on their tails.

Then he went into the kitchen looking very solemn. "I can't bring you any sparrows," he said.

Mother stared at him. "I don't want sparrows," she said.

"But you asked me for some," said Saucepan, in surprise.

"Indeed I didn't," said Mother. "What do you suppose I want sparrows for? To make porridge with?"

When Saucepan and Moon-Face had been at the children's cottage for two or three days, Silky came in a great state of excitement.

She knocked at the door and Jo opened it. "Oh, Jo! Have you still got Moon-Face and Saucepan here?" she asked. "Well, tell them they must come back to the tree at once."

"Gracious! What's happened?" said Jo. Everyone crowded to the door to hear what Silky had to say.

"Well, you know the Old Woman Who Lives in a Shoe, don't you?" said Silky. "*Her* land has just come to the top of the tree! and the Old Woman came down the ladder through the cloud to see Dame Washalot, who is an old friend of hers. And when she saw that Moon-Face's house was empty, she said she was going to live there! She said she was tired of looking after a pack of naughty children."

"Oh, my!" said Moon-Face, looking very blue. "I don't like that Old Woman. She gives her children broth without any bread, and she whips them and sends them to bed when they are just the very littlest bit bad. Couldn't you tell her that that house in the tree is *mine*, and I'm coming back to it?"

"I did tell her that, silly," said Silky. "But do you suppose she took any notice of me at all? Not a bit! She just said in a horrid kind of voice:

'Little girls should be seen and not heard.' And she went into your house, Moon-Face, and began to shake all the rugs."

"Well!" said Moon-Face, beginning to be in a temper. "Well! To think of somebody shaking *my* rugs! I hope she falls down the slippery-slip."

"She won't," said Silky. "She peered down it and said: 'Ho! A coal-hole, I suppose! How stupid! I shall have a board made and nail that up.'"

"Well, I never!" cried Moon-Face, his big round face getting redder and redder. "Nailing up my lovely slippery-slip! Just wait till I tell her a few things! I'm going this very minute!"

"I'll come with you," said Saucepan. "Are you coming, too, children?"

"Mother, Saucepan and Moon-Face have got to go back home," called Jo. "May we go with them for a little while? We shan't be long."

"Very well," said Mother. Moon-Face and Saucepan went to say good-bye to her and thank her for having them. Then they and the four children and Silky sped off to the Enchanted Wood.

"I'll tell that Old Woman a few things!" cried Moon-Face. "I'll teach her to shake my rugs! Does she suppose she is going to live in my dear little round house? Where does she think *I'm* going to live? In her Shoe, I suppose!"

The children couldn't help feeling rather excited as they ran to the Tree. They climbed up it quickly and at last came to Moon-Face's door. It was shut. Moon-Face banged on it so loudly that the door shook.

The door flew open and a cross-faced old woman glared out.

"Do you want to break my door down?" she cried.

"'Tisn't your door!" shouted Moon-Face. "It's mine."

"Well, I've taken this house now," said the Old Woman. "I'm tired of all those naughty children, and I don't want to live in a shoe any more. I'm going to live by myself and have a good time. Dame Washalot is an old friend of mine and she and I will have lots of chats about old times." She slammed the door in the faces of everyone.

Moon-Face peered in at the window. He groaned. "She's nailed up the Slippery-Slip," he said. "She's put my bed across the board she's nailed there. Whatever am I to do?"

"*I'll* see if I can do something," said the old Saucepan Man unexpectedly. "You're a good friend of mine, Moon-Face, and I'd like to do something for you."

Saucepan began to clash his pans together and make a fearful noise. He shouted at the top of his voice: "Come out, you naughty Old Woman! Come out and let Moon-Face have his house! Your children are hungry!"

Now he was making such a tremendous noise that he didn't notice old Dame Washalot coming up the tree looking as black as thunder. She glared at the little company outside Moon-Face's house. She was short-sighted and she didn't see who they were. She thought that they were seven of the Old Woman's children who had come down from the Land above and were making themselves a nuisance.

"I'll teach you to shout and scream like that!" said Dame Washalot in a fierce voice—and before anyone quite knew what was happening they were all taken up one by one in Dame Washalot's strong arms and flung right up through the hole in the cloud into the Land of the Old Woman Who Lived in a Shoe!

And there they were, in a new and strange land again, out of breath and most astonished. How they stared round in surprise!

XIX

THE LAND OF THE OLD WOMAN

The children and the others were most surprised at being thrown up the ladder, through the hole in the cloud and into such a funny land.

It was quite small, not much larger than a big garden. It had a high wall all round to prevent the children from falling off the edge of the Land. In the very middle was a most peculiar thing.

"It's the Shoe!" said Jo. "Golly! I never imagined such a big one, did you?"

Everyone stared at the Shoe. It was as big as an ordinary house, and had been made very cleverly indeed into a cottage. Windows were let into the side, and a door had been cut out. A roof had been put on, and chimneys smoked from it. A rose tree climbed about it, and honeysuckle covered one side.

"So that's the Shoe where those naughty children live?" said Bessie, quite excited. "I never thought it would be quite like that. However did the Old Woman get such a big one?"

"Well, it once belonged to a giant, you know," said Silky. "The Old Woman did him a good turn, and asked him for an old boot. She had so many children that she couldn't get an ordinary house. So the giant gave her one of his biggest boots, and she got her brother to make it into a house."

"Look at all those children!" said Moon-Face. "They're not very well behaved!"

About twenty boys and girls were playing round the house. They shouted and screamed, and they fought and punched one another.

"I don't wonder the Old Woman wouldn't allow them bread with their soup, and whipped them and sent them to bed," said Silky. "They deserved it!"

The children suddenly saw Jo and the others and ran up to them. They pulled Bessie's hair. They tugged at Saucepan's kettles. They made fun of Moon-Face's round face. They dug Jo in the middle and pulled Dick's ears. They were very naughty and unkind.

"Now just you stop all this," said Moon-Face, looking fierce. "If you don't, I'll fetch the Old Woman."

"She isn't here, she isn't here!" shouted the naughty children, dancing round in delight. "She says she's going to go right away and leave us, and we're glad, glad, GLAD! Now we shall have bread with our soup—and we'll go to the larder and open tins of pineapple and bottles of cherries! We'll sleep out of doors if we like, and we'll go to the wardrobe and take out the Old Woman's best clothes to dress up in!"

"Whatever would she say to that?" said Bessie in horror, thinking what her own mother would say if she went to her cupboard and dressed up in her Sunday frocks!

"Oh, she would be SIMPLY FURIOUS!" cried the children. "But she's gone, so she won't know. Oh, we'll have a grand time now!"

One of the children in the Shoe called to the others. "Hie! I've opened a tin of pineapple! Come and taste it! It's lovely!"

With screams of joy the children rushed to the Shoe. Jo looked at the others. "I've just got an idea," he said. "What about telling the Old Woman about the children dressing up in her best clothes? She might rush back here then to get her precious clothes, and we could slip down the ladder, go to Moon-Face's house and bolt the door on the inside."

"That's a really good idea," said Silky. "Jo, you go down and tell her."

Jo was rather nervous about it. Nobody really wanted to go and see the fierce old lady again. At last Dick said he would. He badly wanted to make up for all the silly things he had done a few days before.

"I'll go," he said. And down the ladder he went. He banged hard at Moon-Face's door. The Old Woman opened it.

"Old Woman, do you want your best clothes?" began Dick. "Because if . . ."

"My best clothes! I'd forgotten all about them!" cried the Old Woman. "Those children will be messing about with them. Boy, go to my wardrobe, get out all my clothes and bring them down here. You shall have a sweet if you do."

"Well, I think . . ." began Dick. But the Old Woman wouldn't listen to him. She pushed him away and cried, "Go now! Don't stop to argue with me. Go at once!"

Dick ran up the ladder. He waited there a minute or two, his head sticking out into the Land above. He saw the naughty children coming out of the Shoe dressed up in the Old Woman's clothes, squealing with laughter, and *how* funny they looked dressed up in long skirts and shawls and bonnets! Dick grinned to himself and slipped down the ladder again. He banged at the door.

"Well, have you brought my clothes?" asked the Old Woman, opening the door. "You naughty boy, you haven't."

"Please, Old Woman, I couldn't bring them," said Dick in his most polite voice. "You see, your children have got them all out of your wardrobe and they're dancing about, wearing them – and they've opened your tins of pineapple – and they're going to pull their beds out of doors and sleep there – and . . ."

"Oh! Oh! The bad, naughty creatures!" cried the Old Woman.

She gathered up her black skirts and climbed the ladder at top speed. She appeared in the Land above and saw at once her naughty children dancing about in her best Sunday clothes. She broke a stick from a nearby tree and ran after the surprised children.

"So you thought you could do what you liked, did you?" she cried. "You thought I would never come back? Well, here I am, and I'll soon show you how to be sorry!"

She was so angry that she rushed round like a whirlwind. The children dragged off the clothes in fright, and ran away like hares. The Old Woman ran after them, so angry that she didn't notice that Jo and the others were not her own children. They got whirled in to the Shoe with the others. There they all were, about twenty-five or six of them.

There was a big saucepan simmering on the kitchen fire. It smelt of broth. "Get the soup-plates," ordered the Old Woman. "No bread for any of you to-night! Mary! Joan! Bill! serve out the plates and then come to me one by one for your supper!"

Jo and the others had plates given to them too.

They didn't dare to say anything. They went up for broth in their turn. The Old Woman ladled it out of the big saucepan. She stared at the Old Saucepan Man when he came up.

"You bad boy!" she said. "You've played a

game with my kettles and saucepans, I see! Wait till you've finished your broth and I'll give you a good whipping."

Poor old Saucepan trembled so much that his pans clashed together as loudly as a thunder-storm! He rushed back to his place at once, spilling his soup as he went.

"I want some bread," wailed a little boy. But he didn't get any. Everyone ate their broth, which was really very good.

"And now you will all go to bed – but first you know what happens to naughty children," said the Old Woman, and she took up her stick. All the children began to howl and cry:

"We're sorry we were naughty, Old Woman! We didn't mean to dress up in your clothes!"

"Oh, yes, you did," said the Old Woman. She beckoned to Dick. "Come here, you bad boy!"

Dick got up. He whispered to the others. "Look, I'll let her spank me, and whilst she's doing it you creep out and run to the ladder. Hurry! I'll join you as soon as I can."

Dick went boldly up to the Old Woman.

"Hold out your hands!" she said.

Spank, spank! Poor Dick, he didn't like it at all. He began to howl as loudly as he could so that the others could creep away without being heard. One by one they slipped out of the door and rushed to the hole, looking for the ladder that led down to the Faraway Tree.

"I say! I believe this Land is just about to move!" said Moon-Face, looking round. A peculiar wind had just got up and was blowing round them. Very often when the strange Lands at the top of the tree began to move away, this queer wind blew.

"Well, quick, let's get down the ladder!" cried Silky. "We don't want to live in the Land of the Old Woman! I should just hate that!"

They all scrambled down the ladder, glad to be on the broad branch at the bottom. When they were safely there Bessie began to cry.

"Poor Dick will be left behind," she sobbed.

Everyone looked very sad. The Land above the cloud began to make a strange noise.

"It's moving on," said Moon-Face. "We'll never see Dick again."

But just at that moment someone came slipping and sliding down the ladder–bump! bump! BUMP! And, hey presto, there was good old Dick, in such a hurry to get down before the Land moved right away that he had missed his footing and slid down the ladder from top to bottom!

"Dick! Dick! We're so glad to see you!" cried everyone. "What happened?"

"Well, the Old Woman spanked me, as you saw," grinned Dick. "And then when I went to take my place she saw you were all gone and sent me after you. I tore out–and she came, too. But I got to the ladder first, and now the Land has moved on, so we're safe!"

Moon-Face went into his house, and they heard him banging about loudly. They went to see what he was doing.

"He's taking up the board that nailed up the slippery-slip," giggled Jo. "Good old Moon-Face! I'm glad he's got his house back again for himself. Come on – we'd better go home. We promised Mother we wouldn't be long. It's a good thing we can use the slippery-slip!"

And down it they went, their hair streaming out as they flew down on their cushions. What exciting times they do have, to be sure!

XX

THE LAND OF MAGIC MEDICINES

For a few days the children had no time even to think of going to their friends in the Faraway Tree. Their mother was in bed ill, and the doctor came each day.

"Just let her lie in bed and keep her warm,' he said to the two girls. "Give her what she likes to eat, and don't let her worry about anything."

The children were upset. They loved their mother, and it was strange to see her lying in bed.

"There's all that washing that I had to do for Mrs. Jones," she said. "No, you girls are not to try and do it. It's too much for you."

Moon-Face and Silky came to visit the children one morning, and were very sorry to hear that the children's mother was ill.

"She worries so about the washing," said Bessie.

"She won't let us two girls do it. I don't know what to do about it!"

"Oh, we can manage *that* for you," said Silky at once. "Old Dame Washalot will do it for nothing. It's the joy of her life to wash, wash, wash! I believe if she's got nothing dirty to wash, she washes clean things. She even washes the leaves on the Faraway Tree if she's got nothing else to wash. Is that the basket over there? Moon-Face and I will take it up the tree now, and bring it back when it's finished."

"Oh, thank you, Silky darling," said Bessie gratefully. "Mother will be so pleased when I tell her. She'll stop worrying about that."

Silky and Moon-Face went off with the basket. They took it to Dame Washalot, and how her face shone with joy when she saw such a lot of washing to be done!

"My, this is good of you!" she said, taking out the dirty things and throwing them into her enormous wash-tub of soapy water. "Now this is what I really enjoy! I'll have them all washed and ironed by to-night."

Silky was pleased. She knew how beautifully Dame Washalot washed and ironed. She went up to Moon-Face's house to have dinner with him.

"I do so wish we could help make the children's mother better," she said. "She is such a darling, isn't she? And the children love her so much. Moon-Face, can't you possibly think of anything?"

"Well, I don't suppose Toffee Shocks would be

any good, do you?" said Moon-Face. "I've got some of those."

"Of course not, silly," said Silky. "It's medicine we want—pills or something—but as nobody is ill in the Faraway Tree there's no shop to buy them from."

That night they went to see if Dame Washalot had finished the washing. She had. It was washed and most beautifully ironed, done up in the basket, ready to be taken away.

"I've had a fine time," said the old dame, beaming at Silky. "My the water I've poured down the tree to-day."

"Yes, I've heard the Angry Pixie shouting like anything because he got soaked at least four times," said Moon-Face with a grin. "He's got plums growing on the tree just outside his house and he was picking them for jam—and each time he went out to pick them he got soaked with your water. You be careful he doesn't come up and shout at you."

"If he does I'll put him into my next wash-tub of dirty water and empty him down the tree with it," said Dame Washalot.

"Oooh, I wish I could see you do that," said Silky, tying a rope to the basket of washing, so that she might let it down the tree to the bottom. "Well, Dame Washalot, thank you very much. The person who usually does this washing is ill in bed and can't seem to get better. It's such a pity. I wish I could make her well."

"Why, Silky, the Land of Magic Medicines is

coming to-morrow," said the old dame. "You could get any medicine you liked there, and your friend would soon be better. Why don't you visit the Land and get some?"

"That's an awfully good idea!" said Silky joyfully, letting down the basket bit by bit. Moon-Face had gone to the bottom of the tree to catch it. "I'll tell Moon-Face, and maybe he and I could go and get some medicine.

She slipped down the tree and told Moon-Face what the old dame had said. Moon-Face put the basket of washing on his shoulder and beamed at Silky.

"That's good news for the children," he said. "Come on, we'll hurry and tell them."

The children were delighted to have the washing back so quickly, all washed and ironed. Dick set off with it to Mrs. Jones. Bessie ran to tell her mother that she needn't worry any more about it.

Silky told Jo and Fanny about the Land of Magic Medicines coming the next day to the top of the Faraway Tree. They listened in surprise.

"Well, I vote we go there," said Jo at once. "I'd made up my mind we'd none of us go whilst Mother was ill – but if there's a chance of getting something to make her better, we'll certainly go! One of the girls must stay behind with Mother and the rest of us will go."

So it was arranged that Jo, Dick and Bessie should meet at Moon-Face's house early the next morning. Then they would go up to the strange Land and see what they could find for their mother.

Fanny was quite willing to stay with her mother, though she felt a little bit left out. She said goodbye to Jo, Dick and Bessie soon after breakfast the next day, and promised to wash up the breakfast things carefully, and to sit with her mother until the rest of them came back.

They set off and arrived outside Moon-Face's house at the top of the tree very soon afterwards. Moon-Face and Silky were waiting for them. "Is old Saucepan coming?" asked Jo.

"Hie, Saucepan, do you want to come?" shouted Moon-Face, leaning down the tree.

Saucepan was with Watzisname. For a wonder he heard what Moon-Face said and shouted back:

"Yes, I'll come. But where to?"

"Up the ladder!" yelled Moon-Face. "Hurry!"

So Saucepan came with them and in a little while they all stood in the Land of Magic Medicines. It was just as peculiar as every land that came to the top of the Faraway Tree!

It didn't seem to be a land at all! When the children had climbed up the ladder to the top, they found themselves in what looked like a great big factory – a place where all kinds of pills, medicines, bandages and so on were made. Goblins and gnomes, pixies and fairies were as busy as could be, stirring great pots over curious green fires, pouring medicines into shining bottles, and counting out pills to put into coloured pill-boxes.

In one corner a goblin was stirring a purple mixture in a yellow basin. Bessie looked at it.

"It's a kind of ointment," she said to the others. "I wonder what it's for."

"It's to make crooked legs straight," said the goblin, stirring hard. "Do you want some?"

"Well, I don't know anyone with crooked legs," said Bessie. "Thank you all the same. If I did I'd love to have some, because it would be simply marvellous to make somebody's crooked legs better."

A pixie near by was pouring some sparkling green medicine into bottles shaped like bubbles. The children and the others watched. It made a funny singing noise as it went in.

"What's that for?" asked Jo.

"Whoever takes this will always have shining eyes," said the Pixie. "Shining, smiling eyes are the loveliest eyes in the world. Is it this medicine you have come for?"

"Well, no, not exactly," said Jo. "I'd like to have some, though."

"Oh, your eyes *are* smiley eyes," said the pixie, looking at him. "This is for sad people, whose eyes have become dull. Come to me when you are an old man and your eyes cannot see very well. I will give you plenty then."

"Oh," said Jo. "Well, I shan't be here then! I've only just come on a short visit!"

Dick called to the others. "I say, look!" he cried. "Here's some simply marvellous pills! Watch them being made!"

Everyone watched. It was most astonishing to see. First of all the pills were enormous—as large as footballs. A goblin blew on them with a pair of bellows out of which came green smoke, and they at once went down to the size of a cricket-ball. He then splashed them with what looked like moonlight from a watering-can. They went as small as marbles.

Then he blew on them gently—and they went as small as green peas, and each one jumped into a pill-box with a ping-ping-ping till the box was full.

"What are they for?" asked Dick.

"To make short people tall," said the goblin. "Some people hate being short. Well, these pills are made of big things – the shadow of a mountain – the height of a tree – the crash of a thunderstorm – things like that – and they have the power of making anything or anyone grow."

"Could I have some?" asked Dick eagerly.

"Take a boxful," said the goblin. Dick took it. He read what was written on the lid.

"GROWING PILLS. ONE TO BE TAKEN THREE TIMES A DAY."

Now Dick was not very tall for his age and he had always wanted to be big. He looked longingly at the pills. If he took three at once, maybe he would grow taller. That would be fine!

He popped three of the pills into his mouth. He sucked them. They tasted so horrid that he swallowed them all in a hurry!

And goodness, WHAT a surprise when the others turned to speak to Dick. He was taller than their father! He was as tall as the ceiling in their cottage! He towered above them, looking down on them in alarm, for he hadn't expected to grow quite so much, or quite so quickly!

"Dick! You've been taking those Growing Pills!" cried Jo. "Just the sort of stupid thing you *would* do! You're enormous! How in the world do you think you'll ever get down the hole in the cloud?"

"Oh, do something to help me!" begged Dick, who really was frightened to be so enormous. Everyone else looked so small. "Jo, Moon-Face – what can I do? I'm still growing! I'll burst out of the roof in a minute!"

The goblins and pixies around suddenly noticed how fast Dick was growing. They began to shout and squeal.

"He'll break through the roof! He'll bring it down on top of us! Quick, stop him growing!"

XXI

SOME PECULIAR ADVENTURES

Dick was enormously tall. He had to bend down so that his head wouldn't touch the roof. The little people in the medicine factory rushed about, yelling and shouting.

"Fetch a ladder! Climb up it and give him some Go-Away Pills! Quick, quick!"

Somebody got a ladder and leaned it up against poor Dick.

A pixie ran up it on light feet. He carried a box of pills. He shouted to Dick:

"Open your mouth!"

Dick opened his mouth. The pixie meant to throw one pill inside, but in his excitement he threw the whole box. Dick swallowed it!

And at once he began to grow small again! Down he went and down and down. He got to his own size and grinned with delight. But he didn't stop there. He went smaller and smaller and smaller—and at last he couldn't be seen! It was a terrible shock to everyone.

"He's gone!" said Bessie in horror. "He's so

small that he can't be seen! Dick! Dick! Where are you?"

A tiny squeak answered her from under a big chair. Bessie bent down and looked there. She couldn't see a thing.

"Listen, Dick," she said. "I've got a pill box here. Come running over to me and put yourself in it. Then we shall at least know where you are, even if we can't see you. And maybe we can get you right if only we've got you safely somewhere."

A tiny squeaking sound came from the pill box after a minute, so Bessie knew that Dick had done as he had been told and got into the box. But she couldn't see anyone there at all. She put on the lid, afraid that Dick might fall out.

She stood up and stared round at the wondering little folk there. "What can we do for someone gone too small?" she asked. "Haven't you any medicine for that?"

"It will have to be very specially made," said a Pixie. "We can't give him the Grow-Fast Mixture because he's really too small for that. We'll have to prepare a special little bath of powerful medicine, and get him to go into it. Then maybe he will grow back to his own size. But he shouldn't have meddled with our magic medicine. It's dangerous."

"Dick's so silly," said Jo. "He always seems to get himself and other people into trouble! I do hope you can make him right again. I wouldn't want him to live in a pill box all his life."

"We'll do our best to get him right," said the

little folk, and they began to shout here and there, calling for the most peculiar things to make the bath for Dick.

"The whisk of a mouse's tail!" cried one.

"The sneeze of a frog!" cried another.

"The breath of the summer wind!" cried a third. And as the children watched small goblins came running with little boxes and tins.

"What queer things their medicines are made of!" said Jo. "Well, let's leave them to it, shall we? I'd like to wander round this big factory a bit more. Come on, Saucepan."

Saucepan was very deaf because there was such a noise going on all the time. Fires were sizzling under big pots. Medicines were being poured into bottles with gurgles and splashes. Pans were being stirred with a clatter. Saucepan couldn't hear a word that was said—and it was because of that that he made his great mistake.

He stopped by a goblin who was pouring a beautiful blue liquid into a little jar. It shone so brightly that it caught Saucepan's eye at once.

"That's lovely," he said to the goblin. "What's it for?"

"To make a nose grow," said the goblin.

"To make a rose grow!" said Saucepan in delight. "Oh, I'd like some of that. If I had that I could make roses grow on the Faraway Tree all round Mister Watzisname's branch. He *would* like that!"

"I said to make a NOSE grow!" said the goblin.

"I heard you the first time," said Saucepan.

"It would be lovely to be able to grow roses. Do I have to drink it?"

"Yes – if you want your nose to grow," said the goblin, looking at Saucepan's nose.

Saucepan kept on hearing him wrong. He felt quite certain that the beautiful medicine was to make roses grow. He thought that if he drank it he would be able to make roses grow anywhere! That would be marvellous. So he took a jar of the medicine and drank it all up before the goblin could stop him.

"Now I'll make the roses grow out of my kettles and pans!" said Saucepan, pleased. "Grow, roses, grow!"

But they didn't grow, of course. It was his poor old nose that grew! It suddenly shot out, long and pink, and Saucepan stared at it in surprise.

The others looked at him in amazement.

"Saucepan! What has happened to your nose?" cried Jo. "It's as big as an elephant's trunk!"

"He *would* drink it!" said the goblin in dismay. showing the children the empty jar. "I told him it was to make a nose grow – but he kept on saying it was to grow roses, not noses. He's quite mad."

"No, he's just deaf," said Jo. "Oh, poor old Saucepan! He'll have to tie his nose round his waist soon. It's down to his feet already!"

"I can cure it," said the goblin with a grin. "I've got a disappearing medicine. I'll just rub his nose with it till it disappears back to the right size. I think you ought to watch him a bit, if he goes about hearing things all wrong goodness knows what may happen to him!"

Saucepan was crying tears that rolled down his funny long nose. The goblin took a box of blue ointment and began to rub the end of Saucepan's nose with it. It disappeared as soon as the ointment touched it. The goblin worked hard, rubbing gradually all up the long nose until there was nothing left but Saucepan's own pointed nose. Then he stopped rubbing.

"Cheer up!" he said. "It's gone, and only your own nose is left. My, you did look queer! I've never seen anyone drink a whole bottle of that nose medicine before!"

A shout came from behind the watching children. "Where's that tiny boy in the pill box? We've got the bath ready for him now."

Everyone rushed to where there was a tiny bath filled with steaming yellow water that smelt of cherries. Bessie took the pill box from her pocket and opened it.

A squeaking came from the box at once. Dick was still there, too small to be seen! But, thank goodness, his voice hadn't quite disappeared, or the others would never have known if he was there or not!

"Get into this bath, Dick," said Bessie. "You will soon be all right again then."

There came the tiniest splash in the yellow water. It changed at once to pink. A squeaking came from the bath and bubbles rose to the surface. Then suddenly the children could see Dick! At first it was a bit misty and cloudy – then gradually the mist thickened and took the shape of a very, very small boy.

"He's coming back, he's coming back!" cried Jo. "Look, he's getting bigger!"

As Dick grew bigger, the bath grew, too. It was most astonishing to watch. Soon the bath was as big as an ordinary bath, and there stood Dick in it, his own size again, his clothes soaked with the pink water. He grinned at them through the steam.

"Just the same old cheerful Dick!" said Bessie gladly. "Oh, Dick, you gave us such a fright!"

"Step out of the bath, quick!" cried the pixie nearby. "You're ready to be dried!"

Dick jumped out of the bath – just in time, too, for it suddenly folded itself up, grew a pair of wings, and disappeared out of a big window near by!

"Dry him!" cried the pixie, and threw some strange towels to the children and Moon-Face. They seemed to be alive and were very warm. They rubbed themselves all over Dick, squeezing his clothes as they rubbed, until in a few minutes he was perfectly dry. But his clothes were rather a curious pink colour.

"That can't be helped," said the pixie. "That always happens."

"Well, I suppose I look a bit funny, but I don't mind," said Dick. "Golly, that was a queer adventure."

"A bit too queer for me!" said Jo. "Now see you don't get into any more trouble, Dick, or

I'll never bring you into any strange land again. I never knew anyone like you for doing things you shouldn't. Now, look here everyone – I vote we try and get some medicine for Mother, and then we'll go. Fanny is waiting patiently for us to go back, and I really think we'd better go before Dick or Saucepan do anything funny again."

"What medicine do you want?" asked a goblin kindly. "What is wrong with your mother?"

"Well, we really don't know," said Dick. "She just lies in bed and looks white and weak, and she worries dreadfully about everything."

"Oh, well, I should just take a bottle of Get-Well Medicine," said the Goblin. "That will be just the thing."

"It sounds fine," said Jo. The goblin poured a bubbling yellow liquid into a big bottle and gave it to Jo. He put it carefully into his pocket.

"Thank you," he said. "Now, come along everyone. We're going."

"Oh, Jo – there's a medicine here for making teeth pearly," said Saucepan, pulling at Jo's arm. "Just let me take some."

"Saucepan, that's for making hair CURLY!" said Jo. "You've heard wrong again. Don't try it. Do you want curls growing down to your feet? Now take my arm and don't let go till we're safely back in the Tree. If I don't look after you, you'd have a nose like an elephant's, curly hair down to your toes, and goodness knows what else!"

They were not very far from the hole in the cloud, and they were soon climbing down the ladder, leaving behind them the Strange Land of Magic Medicines. Jo was very careful of the bottle in his pocket.

"Now we'll go straight home," he said. "I'm simply LONGING to give dear old Mother a dose of this magic medicine. It will be so lovely to see her looking well again and rushing round the house as she always did!"

XXII

WATZISNAME HAS SOME QUEER NEWS

Fanny was delighted to see Jo, Bessie and Dick back. "Mother doesn't seem quite so well," she said. "She says she has such a bad headache. Did you get some medicine for her, Jo?"

"Yes, I did," said Jo, showing Fanny the big bottle. "It's a Get-Well medicine. Let's give Mother some now. It smells of plums, so it should be rather nice."

They went into Mother's bedroom and Jo took a glass and poured out two teaspoonfuls of the strange medicine.

"Well, I hope it's all right, Jo dear," said Mother, holding out her hand for it. "I must say it smells most delicious – like plum tarts cooking in the oven!"

It tasted simply lovely, too, Mother said. She lay back on her pillows and smiled at the children. "Yes, I do believe I feel better already!" she said. "My head isn't aching so badly."

Well, that medicine was simply marvellous. By the time the evening came Mother was sitting up knitting. By the next morning she was eating a huge breakfast and laughing and joking with everyone. Father was very pleased.

"We'll soon have her up now!" he said. And he was right! By the time the bottle of Get-Well Medicine was only half-finished, Mother was up and about again, singing merrily as she washed and ironed. It was lovely to hear her.

"We'll put the rest of the bottle of magic medicine away," she said. "I don't need it any more – but it would be very useful if anyone else is ill."

A whole week went by and the children heard nothing of their friends in the Faraway Tree. They were very busy helping their parents, and they wondered sometimes what land was at the top of the Tree now.

"If it was a very nice Land Silky and Moon-Face would be sure to let us know," said Jo. "So I don't expect it's anything exciting."

One evening, when the children were in bed, they heard a little rattling sound against their windows. They sat up at once.

"It's Silky and Moon-Face!" whispered Jo.

"They've come to say there's a lovely Land at the top of the Tree," said Dick, excited. The boys went into the girls' room to see if they were awake. They were looking out of the window.

"It isn't Silky or Moon-Face," whispered Bessie. "I think it's old Watzisname!"

"Gracious! Whatever has *he* come for!" cried Jo.

"Sh!" said Fanny. "You'll wake Mother. Whoever it is doesn't seem to want to come any nearer. Let's creep down and see if it *is* Watzisname."

So they put on their dressing-gowns and crept downstairs. They went into the garden and whispered loudly: "Who's there? What is it?"

"It's me, Watzisname," said a voice, and Mister Watzisname came nearer to them. He looked terribly worried.

"What's the matter?" asked Jo.

"Have you seen Silky, Moon-Face or Saucepan lately?" asked Watzisname.

"Not since we all went to the Land of Magic Medicines," said Jo. "Why? Aren't they in the Faraway Tree?"

"They've *disappeared*," said Watzisname. "I haven't seen them for days. They went – and never even said good-bye to me!"

"Oh, Watzisname! But what could have happened to them?" asked Bessie. "They must have gone up into some Land, that moved away from the top of the Tree – and that's why you haven't seen them."

"No, that's not it," said Watzisname. "The same Land has been there ever since the Land of Medicines moved away. It's the Land of Tempers. I'm quite sure that Moon-Face and the others wouldn't visit it, because it's well known that everyone there is always in a bad temper. No – they've gone – vanished – disappeared. And I DO so miss dear old Saucepan. It makes me very, very sad."

"Oh, Watzisname, this is very worrying," said Bessie, feeling upset. "Whatever can we do?"

"I suppose you wouldn't come back to the Faraway Tree with me, would you, and help me to look for them?" asked Watzisname. "I feel so lonely there. And, you know, somebody else has taken Moon-Face's house and Silky's house, too. They have come from the Land of Tempers, and I'm so frightened of them that I just simply don't dare to go near them."

"Good gracious! This is very bad news," said Jo. "Somebody else in Moon-Face's nice little house – and someone in Silky's house, too! Most extraordinary! I'm surprised you didn't hear anything, Watzisname. You know, I'm sure Moon-

Face would have made an awful fuss and bother if anyone had turned him out of his house. Are you sure you didn't hear anything?"

"Not a thing," said Watzisname, gloomily. "You know how I snore, don't you? I expect I was fast asleep as usual, and I shouldn't even have heard if they had called to me for help."

"Well, listen, Watzisname, we can't possibly come to-night," said Jo. "Mother likes us to get the breakfast, and since she has been ill we make her have her breakfast in bed. But we will come just as soon as ever we can after breakfast. Will that do?"

"Oh, yes," said Watzisname, gratefully. "That's marvellous. I shan't go back to the Tree to-night. It's too lonely without the others. May I sleep in that shed over there?"

"You can sleep on the sofa downstairs," said Jo. "Come in with us. I'll get you a rug. Then we can all start off together to-morrow morning."

So that night old Watzisname slept on the sofa. He snored rather, and Mother woke up once and wondered what in the wide world the noise was. But she thought it must be the cat, and soon went off to sleep again.

Next morning the children asked if they might go off with Watzisname. They explained what had happened.

"Well, I don't know that I like you going off if something horrid has happened," said Mother. "I don't want anything to happen to *you*."

"I'll look after everyone," said Jo. "You can

trust me, Mother; really you can. We'll be back soon."

So Mother said they might go. They set off to the Enchanted Wood with Watzisname, feeling rather excited. Whatever *could* have happened to Silky and the others?

They climbed up the Faraway Tree. It was growing peaches that day, and they were really most delicious. Dick ate far more than the others, of course, and nearly got left behind.

They came to Silky's house. It was shut. From inside came a stamping and a roaring.

"That's one of the people from the Land of Bad Tempers," said Watzisname in a whisper. "They're always losing their tempers, you know, whenever anything goes wrong. I just simply DAREN'T knock at the door and ask where Silky is."

"Well, let's go on up to Moon-Face's," said Jo, feeling that he didn't really want to go knocking at the door either.

So up they went, and at last came to Moon-Face's door. That was shut, too, and from inside came a banging and shouting.

"Golly, they have got bad tempers, haven't they!" said Jo. "I'm quite certain I shan't go visiting the Land of Tempers! Let's peep in at the window and see who's there."

So they peeped in, and saw a round, fat little man, with large ears, a shock of black hair, fierce eyes, and a very bad-tempered look on his face. He was looking for something on the floor.

"Where's it gone?" he shouted. "You bad, wicked button! Where did you roll to? Don't you know that I want to put you on my coat again? I'll stamp you into a hundred bits when I find you!"

Jo giggled. "If he does that it won't be much good trying to sew it on his coat!" he said.

Just then the black-haired man looked up and saw the four children peering in at him. He got up in a rage, flew to the door and flung it open.

"How dare you pry and peep!" he yelled, stamping first one foot at them and then the other. "How dare you look into my window!"

"It isn't your window," said Jo. "This house belongs to a friend of ours, called Moon-Face. You'd better get out of it before he comes back, or he will be very angry."

"Pooh! you don't know what you're talking about!" cried the bad-tempered man. "I'm Sir Stamp-a-Lot, and this is *my* house. My cousin, Lady Yell-Around, has taken the house a bit lower down. We've come to live in this tree."

"But don't you belong to the Land of Tempers?" asked Jo. "Are you allowed to leave your own land?"

"Mind your own business," said Sir Stamp-a-Lot. "MIND YOUR OWN BUSINESS!"

"Well, it *is* my business to find out what you are doing in my friend's house," said Jo firmly. "Now, you just tell me what has happened to Moon-Face—yes, and Silky and the old Saucepan Man, too."

"Moon-Face said I could have his house whilst he went to live for a while in the Land of Tempers," said Sir Stamp-a-Lot, doing a bit more stamping. "And Silky said the same. The old Saucepan Man went with them."

"Well, I just don't believe you," said Watzisname suddenly. "Moon-Face told me that the Land of Tempers had come, and he said nothing in the world would make him go there. So you are telling fibs."

That sent Sir Stamp-a-Lot into such a rage that he nearly stamped the bark off the tree branch he stood on! "How dare you talk to me like that?" he cried. "I'll pull your hairs out! I'll pinch your noses! I'll scratch your ears!"

"What a nice, kind, pleasant person you are," said Jo. "What a beautiful nature you have! What a sweet, charming friend you would make!"

This made Sir Stamp-a-Lot so angry that he kicked hard at Jo, who dodged. Stamp-a-Lot lost his balance and fell. He fell down through the tree, yelling loudly.

"Quick!" said Jo. "He'll be back in a minute; but we might just have time to pop into Moon-Face's house and see if there is any message from him!"

They all crowded into the little round house and hunted hard. Wherever could their three friends be? It was too puzzling for words!

XXIII

THE LAND OF TEMPERS

The four children and Mister Watzisname hunted in every corner of Moon-Face's house, but there was no message anywhere from their friends.

"I say—that's old Stamp-a-Lot coming back," said Fanny. "I can hear him shouting. Let's get out, quick!"

"We can go down the Slippery-slip," said Jo. But he was wrong! The Slippery-slip was stuffed up with all kinds of things—cushions, boughs, carpets, leaves—and nobody could possibly get down it. The children were all staring at it, puzzled, when Sir Stamp-a-Lot came back.

And, my goodness me, what a rage he was in! He had bumped his head and his back in falling down the tree, and he had a tremendous bruise on his left cheek. He came in bellowing like a bull!

"How dare you go into my house!" he stormed. "How dare you pry into my business! I'll throw you out! I'll throw you out!"

He tried to get hold of Fanny, but Joe and Dick stopped him. "We're five to one," said Jo. "You might as well keep your temper, or we may do a bit of throwing out, too. We're going because we can only get fibs out of you, and it's quite plain that our friends are not here. But you'll feel very sorry for yourself when we do find our friends and we all come back to tell you what we think!"

Stamp-a-Lot was furious. He began to throw

things after the children and Watzisname as soon as they had gone out of the house. Crash! That was the clock. Clatter! That was a picture. Bang! That was a chair!

"Oh, dear! Poor Moon-Face won't find a single thing in his house when he gets home," said Jo, dodging a soup plate that came flying past his head. "Now, what shall we do next? Perhaps we had better go down to Silky's house and see if we can find out anything from Lady Yell-Around or whatever her name is."

Nobody really wanted to see Lady Yell-Around – but they saw her before they expected to. As they climbed down to where Dame Washalot lived, they heard a fierce quarrel going on.

"You emptied your dirty water down on me just as I was going shopping!" yelled an angry voice. "You did, you did, you did!"

Then came Dame Washalot's voice. "I did, I did, I did, did I? Well, I'm glad! If people can't look out for my washing water, it's their own fault!"

"Look how wet I am; look at me!" came the other voice.

"I don't want to look at you, you're a most unpleasant person," said Dame Washalot. "Now, look out – here comes some more water!"

There was a sound of splashing – and then squeals and screams as Lady Yell-Around got the whole lot on top of her. The children began to giggle. They climbed down to where Dame Washalot was standing by her empty tub, grinning as she looked down the tree. Lady Yell-Around was hurriedly climbing down, dripping wet, her shopping basket still in her hand.

"Dame Washalot–have you heard anything about Silky and the others?" asked Bessie.

"Not a thing," said the old dame. "All I know is that that bad-tempered creature who calls herself Lady Yell-Around has taken Silky's house and says that Silky said she might have it, because she, Silky, wanted to go and live for a while in the Land of Tempers–a thing I don't believe at all, for a sweeter-tempered person than little Silky you could never find!"

"It's awfully funny," said Jo, frowning. "Silky, Moon-Face and Saucepan disappear–and these two awful people take their places. There's only one thing to do. We'd better just pop up into the Land of Tempers to see if by any chance they *have* gone there."

"Well, that's dangerous," said Dame Washalot. "Once you lose your temper up there you have to live there for always. And you might easily lose your temper with the cross lot of people who live there. I can't think how it is that these two have been able to leave."

"It does sound dangerous," said Jo. "But I think we could all keep our tempers, you know, if we knew we had to. Anyway, I simply don't know what else to do. Perhaps it would be best if I just went by myself–then the others wouldn't have to risk getting into danger."

But the others wouldn't hear of Jo going by

himself. "We share in this," said Dick. "If you can go to the Land of Tempers and keep your temper, we can, too. We need only go up and ask if Silky and the others are there. If they're not, we can at once come away."

"Well, then, we'd better go now," said Jo.

So up the Tree they went, and then up the ladder through the hole in the cloud – and into the Land of Tempers.

Well, it *was* a funny Land! There was such a lot of shouting and quarrelling going on – such a smashing of windows by people throwing stones in a rage – such a stamping and yelling!

"Goodness! I vote we don't stay here long!" said Jo, dodging to miss a stone that someone had thrown. "Look! Let's ask that man over there if he has seen Silky or the others."

So he asked him. But he glared at them and answered rudely.

"Don't come bothering me with your silly questions! Can't you see I'm in a hurry?"

He pushed Jo roughly, and the little boy at once felt angry. He was just about to push the man roughly too when Fanny whispered to him:

"Jo! Don't lose your temper! Smile, quickly, smile!"

So Jo made himself smile, for he knew that no one can really lose his temper when he is smiling. The man glared at him and went away.

"Well, I can see that it would be jolly difficult to live here without getting angry almost every minute of the day," said Jo. "Hie, there – do you know anything about our friends, Silky, Moon-Face and Saucepan?"

The boy he was calling to stopped and put out his tongue at Jo. "Yah!" he said. "Do you suppose I'm here to answer your questions, funny-face?"

"No, I don't," said Jo. "But I thought perhaps you might be polite enough to help me."

The boy made a lot of rude faces at all of them and then pulled Fanny's hair very sharply before he ran off.

Dick and Jo felt angry, because they saw the tears come into Fanny's eyes. They began to run after the boy, shouting.

"Dick! Jo! Come back!" cried Watzisname. "You are losing your tempers again."

"So we are," said the boys, and they stopped and made themselves look pleasant.

Watzisname went to meet them, and as he went two naughty little boys ran by. One put out his foot, and poor old Watzisname tripped over it, bang, on his nose. The boys stood and laughed till they cried.

Watzisname got up, his face one big frown. "I'll teach you to trip me up!" he cried. "I'll . . ."

"Smile, Watzisname, smile!" cried Bessie. "Don't look like that. You're losing your temper. Smile!"

And Watzisname had to smile, but it was very, very difficult. The two bad boys ran off. The children went walking on, telling themselves that they MUST remember, whatever happened, not to lose their tempers.

They met a very grand-looking fellow, wearing a gold chain about his shoulders. They thought he must be one of the head men of the Land of Tempers, and nobody liked to speak to him. But suddenly Fanny called to him.

"Do you know where Sir Stamp-a-Lot and Lady Yell-Around are?" she said. The haughty-looking man stopped in surprise.

"No, I don't," he said. "They have disappeared, and I am very angry about it. Do *you* know where they are?"

"Yes, I do," said Fanny boldly.

"Where are they, then?" asked the grand man.

"I'll tell you the answer to your question if you'll answer one of mine," said Fanny.

"Very well," said the man.

"Have our friends, Silky, Moon-Face and Saucepan come to live here for a while?" asked Fanny.

"Certainly not," said the man. "I've never heard of them. No one is allowed to live here unless they first lose their tempers and then get permission from me to take a house. And now—tell me where Stamp-a-Lot and Yell-Around are."

"They have escaped from your Land and are living in the Faraway Tree," said Fanny.

"But they are not allowed to do that!" cried the head man. "How dare they? I didn't even know we were near the Faraway Tree. Wait till I catch them! I'll shake them till their teeth rattle. I'll scold them till they shiver like jellies."

"Well, that would be very nice," said Fanny. "Good-bye. We're going."

The others joined her as she ran towards the hole in the cloud. "How brave and clever you are, Fanny!" said Jo. "I should never have thought of all that! I'm quite, quite sure that Silky and the others aren't up here."

"I was awfully afraid of that head man," said Fanny. "I just couldn't speak a word more to him. Hurry up–let's get back to the Tree. Silky isn't here. I can't imagine where they all are. There's something very, very mysterious about it."

They all climbed down the ladder to the Tree, thankful to leave behind the horrid Land of Tempers. They went down to Silky's house and peeped in at the window. Lady Yell-Around wasn't there.

"I vote we go in and have a look round," said Jo. But the door was locked and the key had been taken. Bother!

"Well, I'm sure I don't know WHAT to do," said Jo. "But we simply must do SOME-thing!"

XXIV

A MOST EXCITING TIME

As the children stood gloomily outside Silky's house, a voice called to them from farther down.

"Is that you, Watzisname? Any news of our missing friends?"

"That's the Angry Pixie," said Jo. "Let's go down and talk to him."

The Angry Pixie was looking very miserable.

"I can't understand all this mystery," he said. "I saw Silky and the others a few days ago – and then they suddenly disappear like smoke without a cry or a yell. It's funny."

"We've just been up in the Land of Tempers," said Fanny. "But they're not there."

"I thought of going up there to see," said the Angry Pixie, "but I was so afraid I'd lose my temper and have to stay there always. You know what a temper I've got."

"Yes," said Jo. "You certainly mustn't *dream* of going up there. You'd never come back."

They sat there, looking at one another – and then they all pricked up their ears. They could hear a very peculiar noise.

Boom, boom, boom! Knock, knock, knock! Boom, boom, boom!

"Whatever's that?" said Fanny, looking all round. "And where is it coming from?"

"I can't imagine," said the Angry Pixie. "I keep on hearing it. I heard it yesterday and last night and this morning. It just goes on and on."

Everyone listened. The noise stopped and then went on again. Boom, boom, boom! Knock, knock, knock!

"Where *does* it come from?" said Bessie.

"From the inside of the tree," said Watzisname, listening hard. "I'm sure of that!"

"Do you suppose—do you possibly suppose—that it might be Silky and the others—somewhere inside the tree?" said Fanny suddenly.

Boom, boom, boom! Knock, knock, knock! There it was again!

"I believe Fanny's right. I think Silky, Moon-Face and Saucepan are prisoners inside the slippery-slip. Stamp-a-Lot must have pushed them down there, and then stuffed up the hole with all those things," said Watzisname.

"But they would have shot out of the trap-door at the bottom," said Dick.

"We'll go down and open it and see if anything has been put there to stuff that up, too," said Jo. "Come on, everyone."

So they all went down to the tree to where the trap-door was at the bottom. Jo opened it. He looked inside and then gave a shout.

"This end is all stuffed up, too! These two horrid people from the Land of Tempers have got Silky and the others in there, I'm sure. Look—there's all kinds of things stuffed in here. The poor things can't get up or down. They're trapped!"

"Well, let's pull everything out and set them free!" said Dick, and he tugged at a great ball of moss. But it wouldn't move!

Everyone had a turn at tugging and pulling—but it was no use at all. Not a thing would move.

"They've stuffed everything in and then put a spell on it to make it stay where it is," said Watzisname at last. "It's no good. We'll never be able to move a thing. Look—there's Lady Yell-Around coming back from her shopping. We'll just see if we can't make her do something about this!"

But that wasn't any good either. Lady Yell-Around pretended that she didn't know anything about the stopped-up hole.

"What's the good of shouting at me and asking me something I don't know anything about?" she said. "You go and ask old Stamp-a-Lot. He'll tell you what you want to know."

"No, he won't," said Jo. "He's just as big a fibber as you are."

Anyway, no one wanted to see Stamp-a-Lot again. He was such a bad-tempered person. They all climbed back to the Angry Pixie's house, sat down, and looked gloomily at each other.

"*Can't* get in at the top of the Slippery-slip, and *can't* get in at the bottom," said Jo. "How in the world can we rescue poor Silky and the others? It's simply dreadful."

"They'll be starving!" said Fanny, beginning to cry. "Oh, Jo, do think of something!"

But nobody could think of anything at all. It was only when the woodpecker flew by to go to his hole in the tree that any idea came—and then Jo jumped up with his eyes shining.

"I know! I know!" he cried. "Let's ask the woodpecker to help us."

"But how could a bird help?" said Dick.

"Well, a woodpecker pecks holes in wood to make his nest," said Jo. "I've seen them pecking hard with their strong beaks. They make a kind of drumming noise, and can peck out quite a big hole in no time. If we asked him, I'm sure the woodpecker could peck a hole at the back of this room, right into the Slippery-slip—and then we could pull Silky, Moon-Face and Saucepan through the hole."

"Oh, that really does sound a marvellous idea!" said Fanny, beaming. "Let's call him now."

So they went outside on to a big branch of the Faraway Tree and called to the woodpecker.

"Woodpecker! Come here a minute!"

The woodpecker stared round in surprise. He was cleaning his wing feathers by running each one carefully through his beak. He was a lovely bird with his bright, red-splashed head. He spread his wings and flew down.

"What's the matter?" he asked.

Jo told him. The bird listened with his head on one side and his bright eyes shining.

"Do you think you could possibly help us to rescue Silky and the others by pecking a hole at the back of the Angry Pixie's house?" said Jo, when he came to the end of his story. "You have such a strong beak."

"Yes, I know I have," said the woodpecker. "The only thing is I generally only peck rotten wood – that's easy to peck away, you know. It just falls to pieces. But good, growing wood like the trunk of the Faraway Tree – well, that's different. That's very hard, indeed. It would take me ages to peck a large hole through that."

"Oh, dear!" sighed Jo. "I'm so disappointed. We daren't let Silky and the others stay in the Slippery-slip too long in case they starve. There's nothing to eat down there, you know. Whatever are we to do?"

Everybody thought hard. It was the woodpecker who had an idea first.

"I know!" he said. "I could fetch my cousins who live in the Enchanted Wood in another tree – and maybe if there were three or four of us all pecking hard together we could make a good hole quite quickly. I know I couldn't make one by myself without taking two or three days—but a lot of us working together might do it easily."

"Oh, good!" cried everyone. "Go and get your cousins, there's a dear. Hurry!"

The woodpecker flew off. Everyone waited impatiently. They heard the noise from the inside of the Tree again. Boom, boom, boom! Knock, knock, knock!

"Poor things!" said Bessie, tears in her eyes. "It must be so dreadful inside there in the dark, with nothing to eat or drink."

After about ten minutes the woodpecker came back, and with him he brought *five* others! They were all woodpeckers, with bright, red-splashed heads, strong-looking birds with powerful beaks.

"Oh, splendid!" cried Jo, and he took them all into the Angry Pixie's little house. "Peck away at the back, here."

The six birds stood in a row and began to peck as close to one another as they could. Peck, peck, peck! They pecked so hard and so very fast that they made a curious drumming noise that echoed through the little house. R-r-r-r-r-r-r-r! R-r-r-r-r-r! R-r-r-r-r-r-r!

They pecked hard for about an hour and then stopped for a rest. Jo pressed close to see how they were getting on. To his joy he saw that a small hole had been pecked right through into the Slippery-slip. He asked the Angry Pixie for a torch and shone it through the hole. Yes—there was no doubt about it, the woodpeckers had got right through the tree trunk just there.

"Now you've only got to make the hole bigger!" cried Jo joyfully. "Peck away, woodpeckers, peck away! You are doing marvellously!"

XXV

EVERYTHING COMES RIGHT

After a good rest the six woodpeckers set to work again at the hole they had made. R-r-r-r-r-r! went their strong beaks, drumming away at the wood. Everyone watched to see the hole getting bigger and bigger. Then a voice floated up, singing a mournful song:

"Two kettles for Silky,
Two saucepans for me,
Two dishes for Moon-Face,
We're sad as can be!"

"That's the old Saucepan Man!" said Jo in delight. "Did you hear his silly song? That's to tell us they are all there. Move aside a bit, woodpeckers, and let me call to them."

The woodpeckers made room for Jo by the hole. He stuck his head through it and yelled loudly: "Silky! Moon-Face! Saucepan! We're going to rescue you. We'll pull you through a hole we've made at the back of the Angry Pixie's room."

There was a squeal of delight from Silky, a

shout from Moon-Face, and a clatter of pans from Saucepan.

"We're coming, we're coming!" yelled Moon-Face. "We've got a rope to come up by. We shan't be long. Is the hole big enough to squeeze through?"

"Not yet," shouted back Jo. "But the woodpeckers are just going to set to work again, and they'll soon have made it bigger."

"R-r-r-r-r-r! R-r-r-r-r-r!" went the woodpeckers' strong beaks, and the hole grew larger and larger. At last it really was big enough for anyone to get through. Jo leaned through it, his torch shining into the Slippery-slip. He saw a light gleaming a little way down, and noticed a rope shaking near by, as if someone was holding on to it.

"They're coming up," he said to the others. "They've got a light of some sort, too. Oh!–it's a candle. I can see Moon-Face now. He's the first. And he's helping Silky up. The old Saucepan Man is behind. They'll soon be here! Angry Pixie, put on a kettle to boil some water. I expect they would like some hot cocoa or something. And have you got anything to eat?"

"I've got Pop Biscuits and Google Buns," said the Angry Pixie, looking into a tin. "They'll like those."

Moon-Face at last hauled himself right up to the hole. His round face looked white and rather worried–but he gave Joe a grin as usual. "Help Silky through first," he said.

Jo and Dick pulled Silky through the hole. She looked pale, too, but how glad she was to see all her friends! She flung her arms round Bessie and Fanny, and they all cried tears of joy down one another. Then Moon-Face squeezed through the hole, and last of all the old Saucepan Man, though he had to take off a few pans before he could get through!

"We never, never thought we'd be rescued!" said Moon-Face. "We'd quite given up hope. We kept knocking and banging, hoping someone would hear us."

"Yes, we did hear you," said Jo. "That's what made us think you might be trapped in the Slippery-slip. But Moon-Face, how did you get there? What happened?"

"Wait a minute – let them have something to eat and drink first," said Watzisname. "They must be terribly hungry, not having had anything to eat and drink for so long."

"Oh, we had plenty," said Moon-Face. "We didn't starve. But I'll tell you all about it."

Everyone settled down to hear his story.

"You see, one morning this week Silky, Saucepan and I were sitting up in my house talking," began Moon-Face, "and suddenly we saw two people from the Land of Tempers looking in at us."

"Yes – Sir Stamp-a-Lot and Lady Yell-Around!" said Jo. "*We* know them!"

"Well, they looked very fiercely at us," said Moon-Face, "and they told us that they wanted to leave the Land of Tempers because the head-man was very angry with them about something. I think they had broken his windows in a temper. Well, they had escaped, and they meant to live in the Faraway Tree. They had found out by accident that their Land was over it, you see."

"And they wanted your house!" cried Dick.

"Yes," said Moon-Face. "They had been down the tree and seen that Silky's house was empty, because Silky was up here with me, and had taken that for themselves. At least Yell-Around meant to have it for herself. And Stamp-a-Lot meant to have mine."

"And they said they had stopped up the trap-door at the bottom," said Silky, "and they meant to push us down the Slippery-slip, and then stop up the hole in Moon-Face's room, so that we would be prisoners in the slide!"

"Well, you can guess how frightened we were!" said Moon-Face. "Old Saucepan heard it all because Stamp-a-Lot shouted so loudly. And the clever old thing began to stuff his kettles and saucepans with food from my larder, and some candles, too, and matches – and a rope. I couldn't think what he was doing!"

"So, of course, when we were pushed into the Slippery-slip we had plenty of food!" said Silky, putting her arm round Saucepan and hugging him. "All because Saucepan was so clever."

"He managed to tie the rope on to something so that we had that to climb up and down on if we wanted to," said Moon-Face, "and we found a little sort of cubby-hole half-way down where we could sit and eat and drink. We lighted a candle, and then Silky thought of knocking and banging somewhere near to the Angry Pixie's house just in *case* you might be there and heard it."

"Oh, we were so worried about you," said Jo. "We just simply didn't know WHAT to do! I'm so glad we thought of the woodpeckers. So you're really not very hungry or thirsty after all?"

"No, not very," said Moon-Face. "But some of the cake we brought got rather stale. Woodpeckers, would you like it?"

It was a treat for the woodpeckers and they pecked up the stale cake eagerly before they flew off. They had been very pleased to help.

"And now what are we going to do about turning Stamp-a-Lot and Yell-Around out of our houses?" said Silky. "We can't all live with the Angry Pixie. His house is too small."

Just as she said that there came the sound of shouting and yelling some way up the tree. Everyone listened.

"That's Yell-Around, I'm sure," said Silky. "Let's go and see what's happening."

Well, quite a lot was happening! About eight people from the Land of Tempers, with the head-man leading them, had come down the tree to capture Stamp-a-Lot and Yell-Around! The head-man had remembered what Fanny had said, and had come to find the two escaped people. They had easily found Stamp-a-Lot, for he was asleep in Moon-Face's house, which was not far below the ladder leading up to the Land of Tempers.

But Yell-Around had not been so easily captured. She had seen the head-man climbing down the tree and had tried to escape. She had fallen, and had hung by one foot from a branch, yelling and squealing, because she was so afraid of falling. And the head-man picked her up by her foot and dragged her up the Tree like that, bumping her as he went.

Everyone watched in silence. Yell-Around was squealing loudly in a terrible rage, but nobody took any notice.

"I won't go back to the Land of Tempers!" she yelled. "I won't, I won't!"

But she had to! Up the ladder she was carried, upside down, and Stamp-a-Lot was pushed up, too.

"Serves them right," said Moon-Face. "Taking our houses from us and trapping us in the Slippery-slip like that. Let's go up to my house."

They all went up. Moon-Face was sad to see his house so untidy and so many of his things broken. Everyone helped him to put it right. Then they all looked at the stuffed-up Slippery-slip.

"The spell put on it will be gone now that those two horrid people have gone," said Moon-Face. "We can pull everything out."

So it wasn't long before the hole was free of all the things that stuffed it up. Moon-Face shook out his cushions and grinned at the children.

"Well, everything's all right again," he said.

"I'm so happy. It's lovely to have good friends like you."

"We'd better get home now," said Jo. "We've been away a long time."

"We can't slide down the Slippery-slip because it's all stuffed up at the bottom," said Fanny.

"Well, I'll send a message down to the red squirrel to clear it," said Moon-Face. He whistled to a sparrow sitting on a nearby branch.

"Hey, little brown bird! Fly down to the red squirrel and tell him to open the trap-door at the bottom of the tree, and clear the slide there, will you?" he asked. "Tell him to do it at once."

The sparrow flew off. Moon-Face handed round a tin of Toffee-Shocks, and everyone took one. "Just time to have one whilst the squirrel is clearing out the mess," he said. "Hark! I can hear the Land of Tempers moving off."

Sure enough there came the noise of the Land moving away – the curious creaking, groaning noise that the strange lands always made when they went.

"What Land will come next, I wonder?" said Jo.

"I know what it will be," said Watzisname. "I heard the head-man of the Land of Tempers say that the Land of Presents was due to-morrow."

"Oooooh!" said Moon-Face, his eyes shining. "We must all go to THAT! The Land of Presents! That's a marvellous land! We can all go and get as many presents as we like – just as if it was our birthday! Come to-morrow, will you? We'll all go! I can get some new carpets and things. Stamp-a-Lot spoilt so many of my belongings."

"We'll come!" said Jo as he slid down the Slippery-slip on a yellow cushion. "We'll all come! RATHER!"

XXVI

THE LAND OF PRESENTS

Next day all the four children woke up feeling excited. It was so lovely when a really nice Land was at the top of the Faraway Tree. They had been to the Land of Birthdays before, and the Land of Take-What-You-Want. The Land of Goodies had been nice, and the Land of Do-As-You-Please. The Land of Presents sounded just as exciting!

"I wonder who gives the presents – and if you can choose them," said Fanny. "I'd like a necklace of blue beads."

"And I'd like an enormous box of chocolates," said Dick.

"You would!" said Jo. "Anything to eat, and you're happy! I'd like a toy aeroplane that would fly from my hands and come back to them."

"I shall bring something home for Mother," said Bessie. "She wants a new purse. When can we start, Jo? I'm all ready."

They set off about eleven o'clock, when they had done all their work. They were very excited.

It was so lovely to think that Silky, Moon-Face and Saucepan were safe again and coming to enjoy the Land of Presents with them. Perhaps Watzisname, Saucepan and the Angry Pixie would come, too.

Well, everyone in the Faraway Tree had heard that the Land of Presents was at the top of the Tree that day; and, dear me, what a lot of people were steadily climbing up that morning! Brownies from the wood below, pixies and elves, even rabbits from their holes. The Angry Pixie's house was empty. He had gone already. The owl had gone, too, for he was not asleep in his little house as usual. Dame Washalot was gone, and no water came pouring down the Tree as the children climbed up.

"What a crowd there'll be!" said Jo happily. "I hope we aren't too late. I hope there will be some presents left for us!"

"Oh, goodness! Let's hurry!" said Dick in alarm. He didn't want to lose the big box of chocolates he wanted!

Moon-Face, Silky and Saucepan were waiting most impatiently for them. "Hurry, hurry!" cried Silky. "The Land of Presents goes in an hour! It never stays long! Quick! Quick!"

Up the ladder they all went, talking and laughing in excitement. And, my goodness me, what a wonderful Land it was!

There were Christmas trees hung with presents of all kinds! There were bran-tubs full of exciting parcels. You had to dip in your hand for those.

There were tables spread with the loveliest things. And, oh, the chattering and giggling that went on as people chose their presents and went off with them!

Dick marched up to a Christmas Tree because he saw hanging on it a most wonderful box of chocolates. A goblin was in charge of the Tree, and he smiled at Dick.

"I want that box of chocolates," said Dick.

"Who is it for?" asked the goblin, getting out some scissors to cut down the box.

"For myself," said Dick.

The goblin put away his scissors and shook his head gravely. "This is the Land of Presents," he said, "Not the Land of Take-What-You-Want. You can only get things here to give to other people. I'm sorry. This isn't a selfish land at all."

Dick looked very gloomy. He moved away. How stupid! He couldn't get anything for himself, then—and he had so much wanted the chocolates!

He saw a lovely blue necklace hanging on another tree, and he thought of Fanny. She had badly wanted a necklace of blue beads to go with her best blue frock. He went up to the goblin in charge of the tree.

"May I have that blue necklace to give to Fanny?" he asked.

"Where is she?" said the goblin, getting out his scissors. "Call her."

"Fanny, Fanny, come here!" cried Dick. "I've got something for you!"

Fanny came running up. The goblin handed

Dick the blue necklace and he gave it to Fanny.

"Put it round my neck for me and do up the clasp," she said. "Oh, Dick, thank you! It's lovely! Now – what present would you like me to get for *you*?"

"Oh, Fanny – I'd like that big box of chocolates," said Dick, beaming all over his face. "Would you like to get it for me?"

Fanny at once asked the goblin there for it and gave it to Dick. He undid the box and offered it to Fanny. "Have a chocolate?" he said.

Well, as soon as the children knew how to set about getting the presents, they had a most wonderful time. All except dear old Saucepan, who would keep on getting the wrong presents for everyone, because he kept hearing things all wrong.

"What would you like for a present?" he asked Bessie.

"Oh, Saucepan, I'd so like a frock!" said Bessie.

Well, Saucepan thought she said "clock", and off he went to find the biggest one in the Land. He managed to get one at last and put it on his back. It was a grandfather clock and so large that it quite bent him in two with its weight. Everyone stared in surprise as old Saucepan came up with it.

"Here you are, Bessie dear – here's your clock," said Saucepan, beaming at her.

"Saucepan, I said FROCK, not a *clock,*" said Bessie, trying not to laugh. "A FROCK!"

Poor Saucepan. He simply didn't know what

to do with the clock after that, and in the end he left it in a field, striking all by itself very solemnly.

Then he asked Dame Washalot what *she* would like for a present.

"Well, I need a new iron," said the old dame.

"I'll get you one," said Saucepan. But, you know, he had heard quite wrong. He thought Dame Washalot said "*lion*", though if he had stopped to think one moment he would have known that she didn't want a lion – or a tiger or an elephant, either!

It was difficult to find a lion in the Land of Presents. But as the rule there was that whatever anyone wanted they must have, the goblins managed to produce one somehow.

He got a collar and a lead for it and took it back to Dame Washalot and the others. They all stared at him in amazement.

"What has Saucepan got a lion for?" said Jo.

"Dame Washalot, here is the lion you wanted," said Saucepan, beaming; and he put the lead in Dame Washalot's hand. She dropped it at once and backed away.

"Saucepan! Don't play this kind of joke on me. You know I'm scared of lions."

"Then why did you ask me to get you a lion?" asked Saucepan, astonished.

"I said an IRON, not a LION," said Dame Washalot quite snappily.

"Well, then, wouldn't you like to put it into your wash-tub and wash it clean?" said Saucepan.

But nothing would make Dame Washalot take

the lion, so in the end Saucepan had to take it into the field where the clock was, and let it loose.

"Perhaps it will eat the grass and be happy," said Saucepan.

"Oh, Saucepan – lions don't eat grass," said Jo with a laugh. "Now tell me – what do *you* want for a present?"

"Some more kettles and saucepans," said the old Saucepan Man at once.

So Jo went to a bran-tub and said what he wanted. He put in his hand and drew out four large, knobbly parcels – two shining kettles and two fine saucepans. The Saucepan Man was very pleased indeed. He put one of the new saucepans on for a hat.

Well, it *was* fun in the Land of Presents. Everyone went round getting something for the others. Dick got a toy sweet shop for Bessie. She was delighted. She got a fine aeroplane for Jo that flew from his hand and cleverly came back to it each time it flew. Jo got a new hat for Watzisname with a yellow feather in it. Watzisname got a pair of silver shoes for Silky, and she put them on at once.

"Are we allowed to take anything home for our mother and father?" Jo asked Moon-Face.

"Of course, so long as you say it is for them and no one else," said Moon-Face. So Jo went to where a Christmas Tree was hung with pipes and tobacco and got a grand new pipe and a tin of tobacco for his father. And Bessie got a large new purse for her mother.

Suddenly Jo looked at his watch. "It's almost twelve o'clock," he said. "The Land of Presents will be moving off in a minute. We'd better go. Anyway, we really can't carry anything more! Golly, what a lovely lot of things we've all got!"

So they left the lovely Land of Presents and went down the ladder to the Faraway Tree. They said good-bye to Moon-Face and the others, and sat carefully down on cushions, their presents on their knees so that they wouldn't break. And one by one they shot off down the Slippery-slip and out of the front door.

They heard a curious roar as they landed on the moss outside the tree. Jo looked up into the branches.

"Do you know, I believe that funny old lion followed us down the ladder!" he said. "Whatever will Dame Washalot do with him if he won't leave her! I guess she *will* wash him every day in her wash-tub!"

"Well, he'll wish he hadn't left the Land of Presents then!" said Bessie with a giggle. "Come on—let's go home to Mother. What a lovely adventure! I hope it won't be the last."

It won't, because the Faraway Tree is still there. But we must leave them now to have their adventures by themselves, for there is no time to tell you any more. There they all go through the Enchanted Wood, carrying their lovely presents —what a lucky lot of children they are, to be sure!

THE END